ADVENTURES IN TIME

PETE HARTGRAVES

My Only Regret

ADVENTURES IN TIME

My Only Regret

PETE HARTGRAVES

Kravitz and Sons LLC
204 E Arlington Blvd. Suite B
Greenville, NC 27858

Published by Kravitz and Sons LLC.

ISBN: 979-8-89639-354-2 (sc)
ISBN: 979-8-89639-353-5 (e)

Library of Congress Control Number: 2025917415

Table Of Contents

Chapter 1
The Beginning

Then, we were caught in a time-loop, and the universe began to close in around us while the one remaining… just kidding. I just wanted to get your attention so I can explain the science/social studies experiment that we are in the middle of right now. It is pretty wacky. I am not alone, but I will be doing most of the reporting. This is because my handwriting is the best, and I happen to be the only one who brought a backpack to the cafe on that special Friday.

Before I get any further into our adventure, let me introduce to you our little group – the gang. I, of course, am Billy McFarlen, but I am also known to my friends as Billy Mac or just Mac. I would like to say that I am the leader of the group, but if one of the others is to ever discover these notes, or eventually, this book, they might be inclined to tell you the truth. There is no leader. I have no idea why I just told you the truth myself. The three of us try to reach agreements. And if that isn't possible, which is most of the time, we put things to a vote. 2 against 1, majority wins and rules.

More about me? Well, I am thirteen, and I want to be a writer when I grow into an adult. My dad's family came to this country from Scotland shortly after the first world war. My mom isn't sure where her family came from, but she says it had to have been a nicer place than where my dad came from. I think she says that to irritate my dad, just to have fun with him. Also, at times, I think I might have a crush on Joanne. Oh, yeah, my best friends are Bobby Williams and Joanne Rankin.

Joanne Rankin is the oldest, and I guess the brightest, of the three of us. We joke about her being the brains of our outfit, so maybe that would make her the leader. She is fourteen and always curious about stuff. She is also always trying to enlighten Bobby and me even when we don't want to be enlightened. Oh yeah, she also likes to think of herself as the intellectual one, so she makes us use table manners even when we are eating on the ground. She doesn't know where her forefathers, or foremothers as she would say, came from. She just says she is an American now, which is good enough for her. I think her ancestors came from all over the globe. Wherever she is from, she is the most beautiful girl in the ninth grade. She wants to be a scientist when she is an adult, and that might explain a lot about her mannerisms.

The rebel, freedom fighter, rescuer of the oppressed, and speaker for the down-trodden is Mr. Bobby Williams. He is thirteen, and I give him all of these titles because if he sees something he doesn't like or someone else being picked on or wronged in any way, he tends to jump in and defend, fix, make right, and lift up... you get the idea. He is also the devil's advocate, taking the opposing side just so all angles can be examined before decisions are made. So maybe he should be called the leader of our group. In any case, sometimes Joanne and I have to jump in after him and get him out of trouble, and sometimes we just get him into more trouble. Bobby hates seeing people stepped on, partly because he is such a good person at heart and partly because his forefathers came to America from Africa; they didn't come over on a cruise liner. They were bound, shipped, and sold into slavery.

Once, I asked Bobby if he was bothered that his ancestors were slaves, and he said that he would never forget that part of the past but that there comes a time to move forward and not stay stuck in the past. You guessed it; Bobby wants to be a lawyer when he is an adult. Joanne and I keep telling him that he is bound to go into politics. Of course, he tends to say no, but with a sly smile on his face.

Though none of us are hated by our classmates at school, we also aren't exactly popular. We stay away and afar from any sort of trouble, from anything that would have us in detention, suspension, or worse, anything that might lead to our parents getting a call about our wayward behavior.

Anyway, how we became such a tight group of friends, I'll never know, but it happened nonetheless. The funny thing is that, even with our differences, we always stick together. Like any group of friends, we sometimes tease each other. No one gets made fun of all of the time, and, what comes arounds, goes around; meaning any one of us might get teased by the other two the next time. It's all in fun. But if someone else teases one of us, all of our defenses go up.

Now that the introductions are out of the way let me continue with our adventure.

You see, Bobby, Joanne, and I go to eat ice cream at the Neli Deli Cafe every Friday when school lets out. The NDC is a small hole in the wall, and the food could be better (a lot better), but they have twelve flavors of ice cream, and that makes it alright for a hang-out. My favorite kind of ice cream is chocolate, while Joanne always gets Rocky Road. Bobby doesn't seem to have a favorite. It's like he is always looking for a flavor that might be the best, so he has to try every flavor at least three times before he makes his decision. Or maybe he likes not picking a favorite.

After we pick up our ice creams, we go to eat at our usual spot, the booth beside the window, next to the door. Bobby and I are across from each other, next to the window, and Joanne is next to Bobby. While I am devastated that she doesn't sit next to me, I think there is nothing romantic going on between the two of them; I am sure Bobby would've told me if there were something going on. So we sit and enjoy our treat while laughing and talking about our day in school.

We are all wearing jeans this Friday. Joanne's are blue like mine while Bobby's jeans are black. We are all in tee shirts, though none of them are alike. Mine is a brown shirt with a video game character on the front, Joanne's is a blue shirt with a hamburger on the front, and Bobby's shirt is black with nothing on it at all. He is wearing a thin brown windbreaker over his shirt. He says it makes him look sophisticated. I think he doesn't look all that sophisticated, after all. Please don't tell him I said that, though.

While Bobby talks about the bully in gym class and the things he is thinking about doing to take him down a notch or two, our science teacher, Mr. Valinski, sits down in the booth right behind Bobby and Joanne. It is pretty crowded today, with it being the start of the weekend, and Mr. V. sits in the only booth left in the place. He has somebody with him that none of us recognizes, and they are hunched over the table like they are telling secrets. The man he is with is wearing a black coat and tie and black sunglasses. He reminds me of the secret government agents in a movie I like to watch on one of our cable stations.

I want to say that we aren't really trying to listen to what they are saying, but that wouldn't be true. I am listening because I want to know what the teachers talk about when there are no students around. Later, Bobby will say that he wants to find out if Valinski knows he looked at his lab partner's answer sheet to see if his answers were correct on the Friday pop quiz we had in science today, and Joanne will say she was listening because she wanted to see if there are any scientific insights that she can learn. But, whatever the case, our table gets extremely quiet, and this goes unnoticed by Mr. V. and his guest.

By listening, we learn that our teacher is more than just an educator. He is an actual scientist. He is telling this undercover agent, though, with the way he is dressed, he is anything but undercover, about his development of a time-displacement device. It is hard to get the details with them whispering the way they are, but Mr. Valinski explains that he has found the way for mankind to travel through the fabric of time itself. To bend the material of our present universe, causing it to overlap with a parallel universe, and to jump into another plane without getting tangled... blah, blah, blah...

Yeah, you get the point. It is pretty boring stuff, with all of the technical mumbo-jumbo, but Joanne is really starting to get into the conversation. So, we stay, and we listen.

When it starts to sound like the conversation is winding down in the next booth, Joanne whispers that she wants to get a look at this device. She says she wants to see how it works, and without any thought, she gets up and heads for the door leaving Bobby and me staring at each other. After a few seconds, we realize what she just said, so we both leap out of our seats and run after her.

By the time we catch up with Joanne, we are all at the door to the cafe. Trying to impress Joanne with my chivalrous behavior, I reach out, grab the door, and open it with a sweeping arm that says, "you first," and a bow. Bobby takes the hint and cuts in front of Joanne to go through the doorway first and says, "Thank you, Sir." Joanne follows him out of the door, so my gesture isn't totally in vain, but it does let some of the air out of my chivalry.

Joanne breaks into a run, followed closely by Bobby, and I chase after them, not sure where they are going. About the time I catch up, they have stopped in front of the school. "Where are you going?" I ask. I know that Joanne wants to see the device, but to come back to the school just doesn't make sense. I feel we should find Mr. Valinski's secret laboratory or something.

"If we can get to the school before it is too late, we can get to his room. The time-traveling device is there," Joanne explains while Bobby nods, still out of breath.

"What makes you think he would keep it at the school?" I ask, still unsure why I followed them here at a gut-wrenching run.

"It is... here... Mr. V.... said... so," Bobby explains, still trying to catch his breath.

"I didn't hear that," I explain. "He never said where the device is located."

Joanne turns to Bobby and says, "I'll tell him. You look like you are about to pass out from that run." She then turns to me and says, "He said it was at the school. You probably couldn't hear because you were on the other side of the table. Right as they were sitting down, he said that he had to use an instrument at the school to check the calibration. See, the device is there."

"But, how can we get into the school?" I ask, and before anyone says anything, I know the answer. But Joanne tells me, anyway.

"That's easy," Joanne starts, "Remember the broken door that leads outside from the gymnasium? If Sparky hasn't chained it up yet, we can get in that way." Sparky is the name the students gave to the school's head custodian on the day he put out a fire in the boy's bathroom with a cup of coffee. He was supposed to leave the building when the fire alarm began to ring its warning. Instead, he stopped the fire from consuming the school. Rumor has it that he got in tons of trouble for that stunt.

Bobby begins running to the back of the building before any agreement or vote can take place. I turn to Joanne and say, "guess we better hurry before Sparky locks the door." And with that, we take off after our friend.

We arrive at the back of the gym, and Bobby is waiting for us with the door held open. "Took you long enough," he says as he turns and goes through the doorway. Joanne and I follow him without a word. We all know what we are there for, and the thought of seeing this device that will allow a human to travel through time is very exciting. However, none of us even thinks about getting caught in the school after hours, without permission. We try to not think about the consequences because that would just mean that we are being too careful, wouldn't it?

We get out of the gym and peek down the red hallway. No one is there, so we casually walk to the green hallway. Still, no adults around to tell us to stop, so we turn onto the green hallway and head over to Mr. Valinski's classroom.

The door to the science lab is unlocked for some reason. It is supposed to be locked at the end of the school day. Either Sparky opened it to do a cleaning of the carpet, or Mr. V. asked him to leave it open since he would be coming back to the school later. Whatever the case, we enter the room and move to the front of the room, towards Valinski's desk. We stop at the lab table where the class is shown how-to's before we go to do our own lab work.

"Is this really where we want to be right now?" Bobby asks. "I mean, we could get into a lot of trouble for breaking and entering the school." It is obvious that he feels very uncomfortable with the thought of breaking in, so I get ready to pack up and leave. As he talks, Bobby keeps backing up towards the door.

"You should have thought of that before we got here," Joanne replies, "we could have done this without you. The worst they will do is give us a slap on the wrist. It's not like we're going to steal anything." She takes my hand and begins walking toward the teacher's desk.

I stop her with a pullback of my hand and speak up quickly in Bobby's defense. "This is a scary thing we're doing. I'm not sure if I don't agree with Bobby. Maybe we should leave before we get caught."

"Well, you two can do what you want. This is a once-in-a-lifetime event, and I'm not going to miss it. We are going to watch the first human to ever travel through the fabric of time and space. We can tell our children, and they can tell their children, and so on, for generations, that we got to watch our science teacher use a device to travel back in time; or maybe he will travel forward in time, to the future." Joanne begins her speech, sounding quite irritated with us, but after she gets going, it is as if we aren't even in the room at all. She continues, "Just imagine, going to the past and observing history as it is being made. Not reading a writer's interpretation of what they think happened in the past...."

As Joanne raves on about the possibilities of what can be done for the future, I am about to interrupt her. I want to suggest that we all leave together, so none of us gets expelled for trespassing when the decision is taken out of my hands. Voices are coming up the hallway. And I recognize from the voices that it is Mr. V. and his guest.

"Quick," I whisper, "into the equipment storage area!" The equipment storage area is an oversized walk- in closet with shelves for the placement of lab equipment. The door is rarely locked, so I figured we would duck in there, peek out so as to let Joanne see the time experiment, and then duck back in until the adults leave. Since they are already here, it shouldn't take more than ten minutes or so.

I reach the room first, holding the door open so Bobby and Joanne can enter. As they do, I shut the door behind them as quickly and quietly as possible. Bobby turns back toward the door as he enters, and Joanne heads straight toward the back shelf. Rather unfortunately, the door is thicker than I expected, so the voices coming from the other room are muffled. I really can't make out what they are saying, but I keep my head near the door, just in case.

Joanne comes running over to the door where Bobby and I are standing, and she thrusts something, which could be a cell phone, in our face and whispers, "I think this is what they are coming for. Mac, you sent us to the wrong hiding place. They are going to find us, for sure, now."

Bobby, who must be remembering that I always try to take up for him, asks Joanne in his quietest voice, "What makes you think that is the time-travel device?"

"Just look at it," she responds as she holds it even closer to our faces. Sure enough, at the bottom of the hand-held device are ten buttons with numbers, and letters being displayed, much like you would expect to see on a telephone. But above the buttons are three different buttons. One says 'power,' one says 'preset,' and the third button says 'enter.' Above these buttons are two labeled screens. The top one is labeled 'date,' and the other is labeled 'location.' I have to agree with Joanne. We have run into the room that is housing the time-travel device.

Bobby and I are on each side of Joanne to get a closer look at the machine in her hands, Bobby to her right and me to her left. He begins to breathe rather

loudly as if preparing for an objection when Joanne turns the machine on by pushing the button labeled 'power.'

Joanne gets an excited look on her face when a red light begins to blink above the power button. She says in a still, quiet voice, "Let's see where he's been," and she pushes the preset button. To our surprise, the date screen remains black while the location screen begins to blink the words, 'DESTINATION ONE.'

I hear the voice of my teacher say, as he nears the door of the closet, "in here," and I watch as Joanne's right index finger begins its journey toward the 'enter' button. Apparently, Bobby sees the same thing because we both reach for Joanne's right hand at the same time, hoping to stop the inevitable.

Whoopsies. Too late.

Just as we all make contact, the button is pushed, and everything goes dark. It is as if every bit of light energy in the room is sucked into the device. Just then, it creates a loud pop sound, followed by a blinding flash from the under-side of the device. It feels much like a photographer taking a picture with a flash that happens to be the size of the Empire State Building. I close my eyes, thinking that I may pass out.

Chapter 2
My Only Regret

I don't know how long we have been here. I wake up and hear the crickets. I guess I just figure that Bobby and I are camping out in his backyard, again. I don't move or anything. I just kind of lay there, like I am just waking up from a deep sleep; the memory of that Friday afternoon in the science lab's equipment closet seems like the memory of a detailed but fading dream, one that comes off to be rather determined to leave with no traces behind other than a mere conjecture.

It begins to sink in that the sky is much too dark to be in the Williams' backyard. Even on the darkest of nights, the lights from the city make most of the stars invisible to the naked eye, but here, I think that I can see every star in the sky, almost every galaxy that the universe has ever embraced in its arms.

Also, the crickets, they are way too loud, perhaps much louder than crickets should be. And, without moving my head, I can see that the surroundings are all wrong. I am in a meadow, halfway under the branches of a large tree. It is too dark out here to guess at the type of tree, so I continue to lay here for several more minutes, trying to remember how I ended up in this place. Not too saddened to see the peaceful view before me, I see all around me, breathing in the air that feels way too fresh to be true. But just then, I hear the breathing.

Afraid to look around, I just lay here with my eyes staring straight up at the sky, watching as it lightens in its preparation for the sun to take over its entire existence.

Whatever is out here is just out of my view; it is big, and it is close; two words that sometimes you don't want to hear spoken together. I move no more; I just shift my eyes from one horizon to the other, from one star to the other, hoping that whatever it is may not be too lethal.

As it becomes lighter, I begin to look to my right, hoping to catch a glimpse of whatever is breathing so heavily; and that's when I see it. I know right away that I am not in Bobby's backyard. That is, of course, unless one of his neighbors has gotten a new dog – a big dog, a very big dog. There is what looks like a wolf sniffing Joanne's hair.

She is still on my right side, but with her head laying catty-corner away from me. I almost yell, thinking it will scare the wolf, but then another thought occurs to me. "What if I am too late to save her?" I ask myself. This question is closely followed by some more. "What if the wolf has already killed Bobby and Joanne both before I have even opened my eyes? What if, by getting the wolf's attention, it will turn and kill me next?" But that doesn't matter. They are still my friends. No steroid mutilated mutt is going to have my buddies for dinner.

Without making any sudden movements and no noise, I pick up a stone that I can feel right under my head, and I throw it at the animal, hoping it would just run off to wherever it found its way from. A solid hit… right in the side. The wolf jumps a mile high, but when he comes down, he is looking right at me, and a low growl seems to be coming from his stomach and not his mouth. "Oh, my God, I'm going to die! This is how it comes to an end!"

Terrified, I do what any brave thirteen-year-old would do. I screamed the most high-pitched screeching scream I could ever humanly make. I let loose such a scream that I am certain the entire heavenly host regaled at the thought that a human child could let loose with a sound so loud that it could actually pierce the golden gates of heaven.

At the sound of my scream, Bobby, who has been lying just to my left with his head practically on my knee, and Joanne, both lookup and join me in the song of the scared… the scream of the ages… the Holy tempest of the output phenomenon.

The wolf looks around, the glowing eyes opening wider than ever, and sees that there are three of us awake and shrieking our heads off, and he skirts off, out of sight, with his tail between his legs. Apparently, the surprise of not having just one but three living and loud kids to deal with is more than that big fur-ball is willing to take on.

"Jeez, where are we?" Bobby asks as he sits up. I guess he thought one of us should have an answer. "Did all that really happen? I mean, weren't we just in the science lab. Oh, come on, you guys, What's going on?"

"Then, it wasn't a dream. It really is a time and space displacement device." Joanne is, obviously, not frightened in the least. She stands and begins to look around. Her eyes light up, and she begins to examine the device that is still in her hands.

As her smile brightens her face, it almost seems as if there is a heavenly aura surrounding her head. I realize it is just the dust coming off of her head from the ground on which she was just lying. The eyes see what they want to see.

Bobby, still with a dazed look on his face, begins to stand. He says in a confused manner, "What just… when did… how did we get here…? Where… where… where are we…?" Bobby never stammers; he is trying to talk too fast. If we weren't always together, I might have a hard time understanding him, but we are almost never apart, and my mind is doing the same thing as his, just trying to figure out what happened. There are a few too many questions, yet only one seemingly plausible answer.

"I… we… she… She pushed the button!" I say, trying not to sound too accusatory. I stand and begin trying to wipe the dirt off the backside of my jeans. I want to sound confident, like nothing can get to me, but my voice is shaking and breaking, almost as if I would burst out into a cry. "We're certainly in a different place and a different time."

Joanne stands to her feet and begins walking slowly around my stunned companion and me. I think that she is simply trying to take in our new surroundings. We are in a field with fairly tall grass, and there is a tree nearby that we can use as a landmark if need be. I think that there might be a need to meet here if we get separated, but who knows?

With the passage of around ten seconds, Joanne turns and faces both of us, and I can tell that her eyes seem to be getting a little misty. I am about to try to comfort her, ease her mind, and tell her everything is going to be alright when the excitement that has been building up inside of her comes out.

"It works," she shouts. The misty eyes are a sign of joy and not of fear. Makes sense; nothing scares her. "This is great. We are making history, or maybe we are in history, or maybe we are in the future," she exclaims, more to herself than to either me or Bobby. Joanne continues, "What do you call it when you go to the future? We are making history in the future, which doesn't make sense because history, by its definition, is something that happened in the past, and now it seems it could be happening."

Not running out of steam, Joanne continues to let her excitement flow, "Quick, look around. We have to find out where we are. Or when we are. Isn't this great?" With that question – one that we do not know how to answer – she looks up, utterly freezing for an instant. Her jaw drops wider, and her eyes shine brighter, almost as though they were diamonds from a rare engagement ring. Perhaps it is the reflection from the stars themselves that finds its way into my eyes, or perhaps her eyes are truly shining at the excitement of it all.

Bobby and I have yet to fully grasp exactly what is happening. Who can blame us? It is all happening so fast! "This is impossible," Bobby says while still in a seated position. "A time-traveling device cannot take you to a different time and a different place. This can't be happening."

"Sure it can; it happens all of the time," Joanne bubbles back. "When you go somewhere in a car, you wind up in a different place and at a different time than where you started. I think the time and space displacement device puts out enough energy to somehow transport you where you want to go faster, so it doesn't seem like time has passed at all."

And I cannot stop but think to myself, "How can a car take you back in time?" Finally, I feel that I can contribute to the conversation. It is plain that Bobby and I are feeling the same thing. "But a car can't go back in time, only forward, and a car can't fit snugly in your back pocket."

This is a situation that I am not prepared for at this time in my life. Trying to sound older and bolder, my voice only squeaks. "What will our parents say when we get back home? How will we get back home? Will we get back home? If I'm late for dinner, my mom will skin me alive, especially when she finds out where I've been. 'Gee, mom, I've been traveling through space and time. How was your day?' Let's go back now. Wait, what if we can't go back? What if this thing only goes in one direction? What if we end up being in this place forever?"

As if it isn't too obvious by now, I am panicking in a way that I have never panicked before. I am worried, perplexed, not knowing if I am, in fact, going to die here. Bobby seems more relaxed by now but still takes up my cause. "Joanne, you do know how to get us back, don't you?"

Joanne is still looking at our surroundings, and she doesn't seem nearly as concerned about our situation as Bobby and me. "I'll figure it out. In the meantime, let's enjoy everything we can in this time and place," she says with a very nonchalant tone.

Now, Bobby is to his feet, and it looks like his head is about to explode. His voice is getting loud, "Figure it out. Did you hear any of Mac's concerns? I'm asking because I did, and every one of them is quite valid. Personally, I have to be home by 5:00 for supper. If not, my mom will somehow find a way here and kill me, and I will tell on you, miss."

"Wherever we go, and no matter how long we stay there, we can always return to the same time at which we left," Joanne says slowly. She is trying her best to explain this to us in a way that even we understand.

Boy, do I hate it when she treats us like we can't think! "We'll go back to the storage closet with Mr. Valinski and that James guy outside about to find us. We might want to think of an excuse for being in the microscope storage room before we go back," she suggests.

Listening to my friends have this debate does give me some courage. Not to berate or deride either side, but to try to put a little rational thought into where this conversation seems to be going. Plus, my voice is now back to its usual tenor, and I don't want my friends to think I really do sound like a cat. "But, Joanne," I say calmly, "we have arrived at an important event in history. That means we are in the past and not the future. If we do something to change what is supposed to happen, it might change the future and leave us nothing to go back to; our homes could be gone."

"That's called the butterfly effect. This theory holds that tiny, apparently inconsequential changes can produce enormous and globally-felt repercussions." Joanne tries to explain this, but she can see on our faces that the explanation is totally lost. "Okay," she starts again, "imagine the wings of a butterfly flapping softly near a tree. The tiny gusts caused by that butterfly's wing movement does nothing here, but the tiny movement of the air picks up speed and becomes a bigger and bigger gust of wind until it turns into a hurricane on the other side of the world. A butterfly, how much simpler can it be. Understand?"

The answer to the question is an obvious, 'no,' but without a word, we both nod our heads in agreement, with our mouths wide open, almost as if to say, "Uh-huh, uh-huh...."

"Then," she continues, "we just have to find out what the event is and try not to mess with it. I say we should sit back and observe without getting involved."

"So," Bobby ponders, "we have to find out what's going to happen without asking questions so as not to raise any suspicions or change any current events that could lead to a change in the future, which is really our present."

"No," Joanne answers, "we can ask questions, but we have to be very careful not to give any answers. And, have as little contact with others as possible."

Now I am starting to grasp what they are saying. "This is dangerous," I argue, "It's going to be too easy to change what is supposed to happen. What if one of us steps on a caterpillar without even knowing it, and we kill the great-great-great-grandmother of the king of the caterpillars who leads the takeover of the world when humans have all died. The king would never be born, so we just messed up the evolutionary hierarchy of the food chain."

"I did not sign up for this!" my head goes into a much-awaited rebuttal.

"Now you are getting the idea of why we need to be careful," Joanne says. "But I think we don't need to worry about the demise of the caterpillar kingdom as much as keeping our own time clean of any screw-ups. Besides, Mr. V. said it would be 'very hard to change history.'" Bobby and Joanne spoke this last part together, almost like it was choreographed.

"I didn't hear him say that," I protest, and that leaves the door open for Bobby to jump in with his 'afro- dialect,' as he liked to call it.

"Don't cha' remember, Bro? You was on the wrong side of the table, and you missed out on the tasty scraps. Now ya' gotta do some cachin' up, mon." Bobby sometimes really and truly falls into dialect, and he tries to tell us it is Jamaican. But the dialect isn't so much from the islands as it is Central Comedy Hour. But it catches me off guard, and I begin to laugh.

"Anyway," Joanne says, starting the conversation up again, "I think it will be safe if we are careful."

"He said it would be hard for a time-traveler to change the future, but he said we could influence the people who make history," Bobby says. I think that he is starting to warm up to the idea of being a time-traveler, just a little. Now he knows he can stay out as late as he wants and not be at risk of being late for dinner. "Once we know what the historical event is," he goes on, "shouldn't we just stay far away from the person making history or the historical event itself?"

"Exactly, Bobby," Joanne practically shouts, knowing that she now has the majority vote on her side. "Isn't this going to be exciting? We will get to watch history unfold before our eyes, quite literally."

"But how will we get back home?" I ask, still not quite sure that I have complete faith in Joanne's judgment at this point. She just seems too spontaneous and complacent about this whole affair, and this is not in her nature. She is usually very careful about what she does.

"According to what I've heard Mr. Valinski say, We are in a pre-set historical event," Bobby starts. "When we get done observing this event, I'm sure we will return to our own time," he says without missing a beat. It kind of disturbs me how he changes sides so suddenly. We always agree on almost everything.

"That's right, Bobby," Joanne says flatly... "In the meantime, we need to find a place to hide this device so that nothing will happen to it before we are ready to leave."

Now I'm getting upset. My mind is not made up yet, so it is too early for a vote. I still have time to change Bobby's mind. "You mean we're not ready to leave just yet?" I say sarcastically.

Seeing that I am not convinced and really wanting this to be a unanimous decision, Joanne brings out the 'Secret Weapon.' The emotional approach. Her head tucks down as if looking down, although her eyes are now looking at me and her lips begin to pout, pushing her lower jaw outward and sucking in her upper lip. She also turns her hands backward and crisscrosses them so that she looks as if she is unsure what to do with her hands. And, when the look is complete, she says in a sad baby- talk voice, "This is a once in a lifetime chance, and you would keep me from enjoying it? You would keep yourselves from enjoying it?"

Then Bobby adds, without the pout and baby-talk (he would never be able to live that down), "Once we go back, Mr. Valinski will make sure we never get this opportunity again. Think of it as a mystery. The three of us are the detectives, and it is our job to find out what will happen."

"Please let us see this one event," Joanne jumps back in as if on cue, "You've been in history classes. Now you can live history, Billy."

Bobby is acting a little over-anxious but fair. "I'm game just this once, but this decision has to be unanimous. No 'majority wins' on this one. What do you say, Mac?" When Bobby says 'no majority,' Joanne shows definite surprise on her face, but then she begins to nod her head slowly.

"Okay," I say, finally giving in, "but let's hide the machine." At these words, again, as if on cue, both Bobby and Joanne turn their heads towards my backpack, which came off of my back when I lifted myself off of the ground and is now sitting in the dirt about two feet from my right heel. "And there is no way we are going to keep it in my pack. That goes with me no matter where we go on this adventure."

"That's fine," Bobby says, "let's wrap it in my jacket, and then we can bury it. It really isn't even chilly out here." The sun is not up yet and the temperature might be around seventy-five degrees Fahrenheit. Not too cold and not too hot. Why do I feel like I just fell into a bowl of porridge?

Joanne hands Bobby the time and space displacement device that is starting to look more and more like one of those hand-held digital music pods. Bobby begins to wrap his brown jacket around the device. We all know that this is not to keep the device warm but to keep it dry in case they are not around when the rain begins to pour.

"Joanne," I inquire, "doesn't the name 'Time and Space Displacement Device' get a little tiring after a while? You would think we could come with a better name."

"What about Revenge of the Morlock People?" Bobby suggests. "You know, from that book by H. G. Wells, The Time Machine. I think that would be dope."

"But this is science," Joanne lashes out, "and there are no dopes in science. The name Time and Space Displacement Device should not be changed."

Bobby is ready to get in her face, and I can tell that if I don't do something quickly, this could turn ugly. "Both of you have great ideas. Joanne wants something scientific in the name, and Bobby wants something a little more fun and easier to say. What about the TS Double-D."

"I like it," Bobby counters, but we could make it easier and just call it the Double-D. After all, it is a displacement device. Both time and space are displaced. Also, it makes me think of the Dungeons and Dragons game, and you know how much I like to play that. All in agreement?"

And here is the famous vote I talk about a lot. I know I am going to be the tiebreaker again. Bobby comes up with a good compromise, and his hand goes into the air immediately. Joanne can be a little stubborn, and I want to see which way she is going to vote. I decide to go ahead and vote for Bobby's suggestion of 'Double-D' when, to my surprise, Joanne's hand is in the air before mine. Problem solved.

Bobby raises Double-D into the air and proclaims, "I hereby have wrapped Double-D into its official Double- D case and will now bury it under this tree."

"Be careful, Bobby," Joanne warns, "if you accidentally hit the wrong button on that thing, you'll ...."

"Double-D," Bobby interrupts to make the correction.

Joanne complies, "If you hit the wrong button on the Double-D by mistake, you'll be zapped out of here, leaving Billy and me to fend for ourselves in the past."

"Relax, girlfriend," Bobby says, trying to slip back into what he thinks is his Jamaican accent, "I do have enough common sense to turn this game off, ya' know?"

We all laugh at this, and, thanks to the soft dirt at the base of the tree, we manage to dig a decent-sized hole, big enough to fit the Double-D wrapped in Bobby's jacket inside the hole and get it covered with dirt.

After we finish the storage of Double-D, we are all pretty tired. It is not a typical night that we stay up all night traveling through time and digging holes under trees. So we sit beside the tree and rest before the sun has actually broken the horizon.

After a few minutes of sitting between Bobby and me, Joanne breaks the silence. "Let's figure out where we are." She stands up and turns her head to the left and to the right, slowly, as if she is searching for a sign with a red arrow that says, "You Are Here!" She continues, "I'd say, by the looks of it, we're in a meadow somewhere."

"Nice work, Sherlock!" Bobby says with a grin. "The only way we are going to find out where 'here' is will be to leave 'here' and go somewhere else and find someone who knows where 'here' really is. Let's just hope the person we find speaks English and is not a cannibal."

"Another way might be to find a newspaper somewhere that has the location and the date listed at the top." As the words come out of my mouth, I get the feeling I know where Bobby is going with that remark. I instantly regret that weird and unthought combination of words coming out of my mouth.

"Another thing we can do is just wait here for an airplane to fly by with a banner that tells us when and where we are because I sure don't see any newsstands around here."

Even though I am a little embarrassed by the newspaper stand comment, I know Bobby, and he says things all in fun. But, just to make sure there is no confusion on my part, he comes over to me, wraps his right arm around my neck, and wrestles me to the ground. "I'm just kidding with you. Sometimes that's what best friends do."

"You two need to get up and help me come up with a plan," Joanne says, acting like she is put out by our Tomfoolery, as she likes to call it. "We need to come up with a story to explain ourselves. I'm sorry, Bobby, but if we aren't in the twentieth century or twenty-first century, you may have to say you're our slave."

Shaking his head, Bobby is obviously displeased with this suggestion. "Let's say you're my slave and see how you like it," he replies. "I've always said I will never be a slave to no man. And yes, that's man, as in mankind, because I won't be your slave either, Joanne."

"Okay," I say, "point taken. How about we say you work for us?

He nods his head but still isn't smiling. "Fine, but we say I get paid time and a half for overtime. That makes sense and is more realistic."

"Too twentieth century," Joanne adds. "Would you mind saying that you're our servant?"

"Yes, I would. But, depending on when in time we have landed, I will say I'm your servant if you say I am working to earn my freedom." Joanne and I just nod. It is a great idea, and we both know it.

"And you have to say that you will be giving me some cash upon the earning of said freedom," Bobby adds.

Again, this is agreeable to Joanne and me, so we continue to nod without saying a word.

"And you'll say that when I get my freedom, you will both start serving me for a year," Bobby added again, pushing to see just how far we would go. At this, he stands to his maximum height and looks down at me. We don't mention that Joanne is taller than him.

"Now you're starting to push this point way beyond what anyone might believe in much of our nation's past," I say. "Let's make a deal. If we need to, in a worst-case scenario, we will say that you earned your freedom by saving my brother from drowning, and now we are friends."

"Okay," Bobby finally agrees, "but it might just be best for me to sit back near this tree and observe until we know where we are."

"That's a deal," Joanne and I both say together, leaving it to Bobby to come up with a solution that we can all live with.

Right after we get our story straight, we hear voices coming down a road that is nearby that had, thus far, gone unnoticed due to the darkness. Bobby runs behind the tree, I fall into the tall grass, and Joanne walks out of sight toward the voices. I suppose she ducks in the grass, too, but I can't be sure. I am almost in awe of her courage, or perhaps she cares about satisfying her curiosity more than living a full life.

"Why did you not do thy bookwork, Jacob?" a young girl's voice asks. "Ms. Gilbert will probably not say much, but I assure you that when Uncle Nathan arrives and discovers what you have done, he will surely take the switch to you. Then, the mother will as well. You know the house rules."

"Elizabeth, I did not have enough time," a young man's voice replies. "I went to town to listen to the soldiers. You know Father says that as a loyal Tory, we should always know what the troops are up to so we can lend a hand if they need our assistance."

"Oh, you mean the 'Redcoats.' If you ask me, they have no business being here in the first place," Elizabeth begins. We are getting along fine without them here in the colonies. What makes them think they can boss us around all the time?"

"Be warned," Jacob says with a bit of malice in his voice. "Father has said on more than one occasion that he will not stand to hear talk like that coming from the two of us. He says it is bad enough coming from Uncle Nathan, but he says his children will be Loyalists until the day we die."

"But isn't that our decision, Jacob?" Elizabeth says with her voice rising with emotion. "If he can't do anything to stop his cousin from thinking this way, why does he think he can stop what goes on in our heads? You and I were born in America, and I think that makes us more American than English."

Jacob responds, but his voice remains steady and in control, as if without passion. "But Father thinks we should also be loyal to the King of England. Look at all he does for us, after all."

"What, Jacob? Name me one thing that the English do for us that we could not do for ourselves."

"Elizabeth, the Redcoats protect us from the barbaric natives as well as those heathen French soldiers," Jacob answers dispassionately. "Now, I don't want to hear any more of this talk from you. You know that Father says that if we begin talking like his cousin, Uncle Nathan, he will have to discontinue our tutoring services, and he might even turn him into the Redcoats. I might even tell Father about the words coming out of your traitorous mouth."

"Okay," Elizabeth replies though with an undefeated tone, "but I don't think you are going to tell Father about what I have said. You have called the English soldiers 'Redcoats,' and he says that any good Loyalist knows that it is a term of disrespect."

"Not a word," Jacob says. In his voice, there is a definite surrender. He knows that he has been beaten by his little sister in this battle of words, but there is nothing he can actually do about it.

"Now, Jacob, you must repeat the words you have heard from the soldiers in town." Elizabeth was determined to push this win to her full advantage.

"I cannot. You will tell Uncle Nathan, and we could be tried as spies." Upon hearing these words, Elizabeth's eyebrows arch in surprise as Jacob's head falls down. More defeat. "Okay, fine. That is the word from the soldiers. They know that General Washington has a spy in the New York territory, and he is bringing information to the Patriots. There could be more than one spy. Now, don't repeat this to Uncle Hale, or you could both wind up being hanged."

At this point in the sibling's conversation, just as the voices are beginning to move out of range of my hearing, I hear rustling in the grass ahead of me and know, without looking, that Joanne has arisen and is probably running toward the children as they walk away.

Figuring that someone had better take care of her, I jump up and look toward the fading voices. I then look to the tree that is hiding my friend. Bobby is looking at me from behind the tree with a look of desperation on his face. I simply thrust my arms in a downward motion, palms downward to indicate that he is to stay where he is while I leave to catch up with Joanne. By this time, she is fifty yards ahead of me.

Just then, I yell, "Wait!"

Chapter 3
Splitting Up

Now, when a snowball begins to roll down a steep hill, it gathers more snow, and it gets bigger. As the snowball becomes heavier, the more speed and momentum it gains. Once that snowball is large enough, a person cannot stop it and will be swallowed up by the snowball if he gets in the way. Now you know how I feel. No, I am not the snowball. No, I'm just the person who jumps in front of it.

I neither have an idea what the historical event is going to be in this time period, nor do I know how we are going to find out what that event might be. And I certainly have no idea what Joanne has in mind as she goes running to catch up with Jacob and Elizabeth. But I do have a sneaky suspicion that Joanne knows what she needs to do to find the answers to these questions, so I will follow along and try to help.

"Wait up," Joanne continues to yell until, at last, Jacob and Elizabeth stop and turn to face us. As they turn, I can put a face to the voices I have been listening to in the grass. Both are dressed in the richest of clothes.

Jacob, standing at about five feet, seven inches, looks to be about fifteen or sixteen with short blond hair. He is wearing a long-sleeved, button-up white shirt that appears to have lace at the collar. He also has on black suspenders holding up black trousers that go down to his knees. His leather shoes, dark brown with a gold buckle on top, are very dusty but look as though they get polished regularly. To go rather impeccably with the outfit, as if it needs anything else, Jacob has on a black jacket that matches his pants.

Elizabeth, who is obviously younger than Bobby and me, stands at about four feet and ten inches. She has on a green dress that also has lace around the collar. The dress comes down to her ankles and looks to be fitted with several different layers around the skirt. With that long dress, there is no way I can ever see her feet, but I can imagine that she is wearing the best-looking pair of shoes that money can buy. She and her brother both seem to be lacking for nothing. Perhaps they come from a background that is lavish, or perhaps they work hard and get paid for what it is that they deserve.

Needless to say, Joanne and I are not dressed in any way as to be associated with this class of children. But, here we are. I am wearing my blue jeans with a dark brown pullover t-shirt that has a running flower ironed onto the front. The flower is a video game character. On my feet, I have on my green and white Keds.

Joanne is wearing acid-washed blue jeans and a blue t-shirt. I can see that she has turned her shirt inside- out to hide the hamburger that is ironed onto the front. "Hmm," I whisper to myself. This must have happened while we were listening in the tall grass. On her feet, Joanne is wearing her white tennis shoes.

Now, in the twenty-first century, if strangers come running at you out of nowhere, there is a good chance you are going to be robbed or shot. But since this is not the twenty-first century, I am not sure why Jacob and Elizabeth have such worried looks on their faces. I guess it might have been because they were worried that we overheard their conversation regarding the English soldiers we had.

"Don't hurt us! Please, don't hurt us!" Elizabeth screams as she buries her head into her brother's chest. Even though Jacob is a few inches taller than me, he still has a worried look on his face as we approach. He seems quite pale, almost as though all of his blood has been drained from his head. As I look right into his eyes, I can see that there is a sense of worry and fear that prevails all over and around him.

"We mean you no harm," Joanne says quite breathlessly, her hands raised apologetically toward the fellas, who seem much taken aback. She has the biggest "trust me" grin on her face, and it is very convincing. Maybe she is a member of our group that should run for public office.

"We don't mean to scare you. We just came to town, and we were wanting to get to know you. You know, be friends."

"Where are you from, milady? What brings you to Long Island?" Jacob asks, looking right at Joanne.

"We are from the southern colonies, and our parents heard that the Tories might need help in the New York territories. We were on our way to help when we were ambushed. Our parents were taken from us, and Billy and I barely managed to escape." The strangers' eyes shift toward me and then back at the girl beside me, who continues perfectly with the made-up storytelling.

All the while Joanne talks, I just watch her with a shocked look on my face. Where in the world is she coming up with all of this? I cannot stop but wonder. The thoughts pile into layers in my head, and I cannot find an answer. When the three of us talked about the story that we should tell others to explain our situation, it was never this detailed. How is she doing all this?

"Wow, she's amazing!" one of the thoughts races across my head, and I don't know what it implies.

"Tell me about your attackers," Jacob inquires. "Were they wearing English uniforms, or were they in rebel uniforms?"

"Now and then, both sides act as if they are our enemies," Elizabeth adds.

"Uhhh… we weren't around when the group was attacked," I stammer. "We… were out hunting in the woods for sheep!" I cry out, almost as though a revelation, trying not to sound too pretentious.

"He means we were in the woods looking for some of our animals that wandered off," Joanne explains before I realize you wouldn't hunt sheep, especially not in the woods.

"Are you the only ones who managed to escape?" asks Jacob. "Or were there others who got away with you?"

"Oh, we have a friend," I say, forgetting that I am not supposed to mention Bobby. "I mean, we have someone around here, somewhere. He's looking for the others, but they were taken away… far away. He's not the same as us. I mean, he's colored, uh… he's… well, he is black."

By the look on the faces of both Elizabeth and Jacob, I can tell that I am not nearly as good at storytelling as Joanne is. They both have eyebrows that are going down in the middle and foreheads that are crinkled into a knot. I think that I am doing such a bad job that I will let Joanne clean up my mess. She knows what to say.

"Oh, you mean he's an African?" Jacob inquires. "I've never thought of them as black. Their skin tone is more of a dark brown than black, so I was baffled for a time. Can I see him? I don't get to see them very often. I am a bit curious, to speak the truth."

Joanne steps in like a champ. She is probably terrified that I will blow our story and get us caught in a lie. I am very surprised we haven't been caught yet. "Our friend was with us when the group was attacked, and he said he would track the others and let us know what he finds."

"Do you want me to have my father get the magistrate to look for thy servant," Jacob offers in a sincere sort of way. "I've heard of them running away before, and I guess that is what we are supposed to do in a situation like this."

"No," Joanne blurts out, "We said he is our friend."

Jacob's eyes get a curious look on them, and he asks, "Why do you refer to him as a friend? Isn't he your slave?"

"No," I respond quickly, trying to respect the dignity of my best friend. "He saved my life when I was drowning. He has earned his freedom."

Joanne improvises, "He saved me from a burning barn. He has earned his freedom."

And I decide to take it a step further. "Joanne and I both believe that no human has the right to own another human. Bobby is more human than anyone I have ever known."

"Sounds like you both have a very strong attachment to… your… erm, friend," Jacob says as he tries to grasp the idea of an African as a friend. "I guess he must be a special person to put his life at risk to save yours. I can understand why you are so attached to him. I am sure he appreciates you giving him his freedom. Our servants are not brown-skinned, but my mother says that if you want to encourage their loyalty to the household, you should allow them to make personal decisions on their own."

"But should that not also apply to the colonies?" Elizabeth is back on the subject of the revolting colonists, and I watch Jacob cringe the moment she begins speaking. "Would not this talk of an uprising be more easily controlled if we were permitted to vote for a representative in the parliament? Uncle Nathan says that there is a man by the name of Franklin who would be a superb representative." With an emphasis on the word 'representative,' she raises her chin high in the air and closes her eyes in a defiant gesture.

"Ignore my sister," Jacob apologizes while looking at me. Then, turning his attention to Joanne, he adds, "She babbles on without knowing what she speaks of. I think that there are times when her faculties are not functioning up to speed."

"Humph," Elizabeth snorts and turns her back to her brother.

"Nonetheless," Jacob continues as he turns his attention back to me, "we have been talking for a time now, and I still do not know what I should call you. My name is Jacob, and this is my sister Elizabeth. My family comes here from Lincolnshire, England."

"I am not from there," Elizabeth argues with her back still to her brother, "I am an American."

I am beginning to really like the spunk this girl has. It reminds me a little of Joanne. It also makes me think of the spirit of the men and women who founded our nation.

"Please forgive my sister," Jacob apologizes once again, not knowing that we probably respect Elizabeth more because of her attitude. Her brother continues, "She is not a rebel or a patriot. She just occasionally allows her mouth to run without forethought." It is plain that he fears the trouble that they can get into if his sister is overheard talking the way she is.

A little agitated at Jacob's feeling of the need to defend his sister, Joanne says, "My name is Joanne, and your sister's words didn't bother me in the least. In fact," she says, turning to face Elizabeth and bending down a little so that their faces were closer, "I think all people should have the right to say what they want to say. It is what makes us human, after all, isn't it… the difference of the ways in which we think?"

Hurriedly, I jump in to keep Joanne out of the doghouse. "But we're not Patriots, either." I turn towards Jacob and speak directly to him. "I'm Billy, and it looks like I'm a lot like you. We both have sisters who tend to talk before they have completely thought out the situation." I then stick out my hand and grasp the hand of Jacob while I give a stern warning look to Joanne, who is still bent down with Elizabeth. Elizabeth looks at Jacob with an extremely put-out expression on her face.

The funny thing I learn from listening to Elizabeth on this day is that she has no idea how close she is to the truth about the rebellion and what it is all about. Though I respect her point of view, I really don't think it is all her own. I feel that the words that were coming out of her mouth must be the words of an adult, somebody close to the family.

"So, where is thy birthplace?" Elizabeth says as she turns her gaze away from her brother and toward us. I guess she got tired of staring fiercely at Jacob.

"Huh," I start, not thinking of all of the glaring holes in our story. "Oh, we come from Texas."

"What country is that?" Elizabeth asks. "I have never heard of such a place."

"UH, what my brother means to say is that we come from Texas, in the mountains of Virginia," Joanne says, coming to the rescue and saving our skins again. "It is a small community, but it is a nice place to live. Lots of Loyalists there," she says as she turns once again to face Jacob.

"That's funny. Father says that Virginia is overcrowded with Patriots and that we would be better off if the entire region would just fall off into the sea." When Jacob says these things, I don't think he is trying to be mean. He, like his sister, is just repeating what he has heard from the adults around him.

"There are some Patriots who make a lot of noise, but for the most part, there are loyalists who will do anything for the crown," I argue. I was catching onto this storytelling thing, and it is becoming easier than I had ever hoped it would be – kind of a scary thought for those who know me.

Somewhere in the conversation, the four of us begin walking in the direction Jacob and Elizabeth had been traveling before we caught up to them. I believe it was southeast, judging by the direction of the morning sun, but I don't have a compass, and my sense of direction can be pretty bad sometimes.

It was one time earlier on, while I was riding my bike, that I got turned around and couldn't find my house, and I was on my own street. It doesn't get much worse than that.

We begin seeing more and more houses, and it isn't long before we come to a small home with yellow paint. The trim on the house is brown, and there is a chimney on the right side. The well-manicured bushes in the front let me know that whoever lives here spends a great deal of time taking care of the outside appearance of the house.

"Whose house is this?" I ask Jacob without taking my eyes off the front door. "It is beautiful."

Elizabeth speaks up and says with a little of the attitude I was beginning to appreciate, "A girl is beautiful, not a house! A house is just… a house!"

"This is the house of our teacher, Ms. Gilbert," Jacob says. "She is nice and knows a lot about books, but she has asked my father to find another tutor for us. It seems as if she wants to have more time to work in her garden. Since her husband was killed, she tends to spend all hours of the day in that garden. That is, except when we are here."

"Say, would you like to come in and have a lesson with us?" Elizabeth offers. "Maybe you could start attending the sessions with us until Father finds us a new teacher. I am sure your parents would really like that you are learning with us. And when they are found, they might want you to learn with our replacement teacher, too."

"Do not make them uncomfortable, Elizabeth," Jacob says as he sends an angry look in her direction. He then turns to Joanne and says, as his face turns red, "But my sister does have a good point. I know that you probably have family here to stay with, but, since your parents are taken and if you have nowhere else to stay, I am sure that my father will let you stay at our house. We have plenty of space. Maybe we can even find some clothes for you so you can change out of those rags."

Then, realizing how late it is getting and not realizing that he might have been rude in regards to their twenty-first-century clothes, Jacob begins to run toward the house, followed by his sister, and yells over his shoulder, "We have to go, but we can meet you here later today to discuss this idea." But then he pauses before going inside.

Joanne turns away. She looks as if she doesn't know how far to take this charade after such a pleasant invitation. He actually asked them to stay in his house if they needed a place to stay. She looks like she is going to get choked up, so I say, "We'll meet you back here when you get done, and we can talk about it. How long will you be in with your teacher?"

"We usually go home for lunch and then come back after we eat," Elizabeth says. "But today, we can ask if she will allow us to not attend the afternoon class. Do you want us to see if she would mind letting us go early?" She looks excited as she asks this. Maybe it is because she likes the idea of her brother meeting a girl, but maybe it is because she likes to see her brother get blushed and confused over having met the girl. Who knows?

"That will be great," I yell as we are walking away. But realizing we don't have a watch, I decide to use what is at hand. "We'll come back when the sun is directly overhead."

Joanne turns halfway around to face me and whispers, "Are you sure we can make it back here by that time, Billy? We have a lot to do to find the historical event."

Not hearing the quiet protest, Jacob continues walking towards the house as he shouts, "Then it is settled. We will be done when the sun is at its highest and then we can all go to our house for some lunch. If Elizabeth and I have to return for lessons, maybe the two of you would like to visit with our parents. Ms. Gilbert might even be in a good enough mood to let us leave before our lunch break. If so, we will wait for you here."

"No need to rush because of us," Joanne says in a flustered sort of way. She doesn't sound rude, but there is a tone in her voice that shows things are getting out of her control. "We have things to do, too. This part of New York is a busy place." but before she can finish her sentence, the door to the house shuts, and she is alone with me.

After all the goodbyes are finished, I am finally able to talk to Joanne alone. I turn to her and ask, "How did you ever find out we are in New York? What did I miss? Do you know something from the history book that I didn't learn?"

"Are you kidding? How could you have missed it?" she asks in a condescending tone. "They said they were in Long Island. I never would have picked that up from their accents, but finally, it dawned on me. As soon as I knew where they were from, I knew I could strike up a conversation with them."

"But you were so convincing," I insist, still amazed at how gracefully she handled the story. "How were you able to just pull a story like that out of thin air? That wasn't even the story that we had discussed."

"It wasn't hard," she explains. "As soon as I realized that the issue in this time period wasn't slavery, I knew that the story we had come up with probably wouldn't float. I still can't believe you told them that Bobby was out there. Now they will be looking for him."

"Ah, they probably won't even give it a second thought," I say, hoping and praying to all of the powers that be that I am correct. God, luck, fate; I have to be right.

"And even considering staying with them," she adds. Now I am a real thorn in her side. "Have you lost your ever-loving mind? Bobby is out there, and we need to stay in contact with him to make sure everything is okay: not to mention the fact that we have an important event in history to discover. Don't you think that hanging out with these two might slow us down just a tad?"

"We have a place to stay," I explain, "and you have to admit that we have no way to get any food and no place to sleep. I think that this could be a good thing."

"That may be fine for us," she says sarcastically. "But what about our escaped slave? How will he get food, and where will he sleep? I think we should stick together through thick and thin."

She is definitely making a good point. We both love Bobby. He is my best friend, but in the thick of the conversation, I have not even thought about his well- being.

"You are right, as usual, but maybe if we are staying at the house, we can sneak him things to eat," I say, trying to defend my idea. "I hate the thought of splitting up, same as you, but it might become necessary. We have got to get out and talk to the locals, especially the grown-ups. That might be easier to do if we can get on the inside. We have to get people to trust us."

"You might be right, but we should really leave this decision up to Bobby. After all, he is going to be the one we end up leaving out in the cold." Joanne seems to be warming up to the idea a little, but I am also starting to see her point and how Bobby might feel.

And so, I walk away from the house along with Joanne, trying to figure out the way in which we had come up until here. But it seems Joanne has it figured out. She knows the way. I walk beside her, "After you, milady."

CHAPTER 4
SCARED? NOT ME

Joanne and I head off in search of Bobby. Joanne has a good sense of where we are, but I seem to have a hard time trusting her instincts. How can she possibly know where we are going when can she possibly know where we are going when there is nothing certain about the place? I am wondering, trying to go in the opposite direction, and I hear her whispering to me, "This way; I remember this tree," or, "You're going to get me confused. I think I know where I am going, so just follow me."

When we get to the tree where we left Bobby, he is not to be found there. We look all around the area surrounding the tree, but he is nowhere to be found. I notice a group of trees on the rise in the terrain and think it almost looks as if the trees are on the horizon of the meadow. They might have been an entrance to a grand forest, for all I know about the area. "What if Bobby's been taken by an Indian or maybe chased away by a wild animal?" Joanne asks. "Where could he have gone?"

"Well," I say, after surveying the area another time. I am determined not to get lost again. "That could have happened, but I don't think we really should be jumping the gun on this. We really need to examine all possibilities before we begin to panic. For instance, those trees up the hill, on the horizon. I had not paid any attention to them when we were here before. Maybe Bobby saw them and decided to go look for food. Anything could have happened, so let's not ponder over the worst?"

Joanne interrupts my last sentence with an emotional outburst. "Maybe something or somebody chased him over there." As she speaks, fear begins to grip me, and I start to run in the direction of the cluster of trees. I know what is important to me, and proudly, I can say that nothing surpasses friendship. Still fearful, the worst of thoughts and possibilities parading around my head, I don't even stop to realize that I have left Joanne behind, speaking the last words of her sentence. Then I see that she is running right beside me, maybe even a little ahead of me.

We get to the trees, and I realize that this is no forest. It is merely a band of trees that have grown around a small stream or a creek. The trees look to be tall oak trees, but I couldn't tell you what kind of oak. This surprises me because all of the trees appear to be of the same kind, and there don't appear to be any others around – how very unusual! I would have expected some different varieties to be around the area.

As Joanne and I start to walk quietly into the band of trees, we begin to hear something tapping on wood, some sound that seems to be too unfamiliar, yet in a pattern, as though we are being called toward. At first, it appears to come from more than one place in the area, then it seems to be completely surrounding us as if we have walked into a bowl of sound, bouncing off the opposite side and coming back at us; reverberating ceaselessly, with the single purpose; to drive us crazy.

Trying to locate the origin of the sound by now is impossible. I grab Joanne's hand in case she is scared, or, just maybe, in case I am scared. Finally, when I am ready to suggest to Joanne that we try to find Bobby in another location, like anywhere outside of this spooky band of trees, a loud noise comes from above us. Before I can look up and focus on what is there, something large topples on top of Joanne and me and takes us both to the dirt.

"What do you mean, leaving me here, by myself, for such a long time?" Bobby hollers, too abysmal, too worried, as though he is shaken. "Do you know how scared I was without you here? I didn't know if something had happened to you, and how could I leave this time period without you, without knowing if you were still alive or not? Have you no shame?!"

"We're so sorry," Joanne apologizes as she throws her arms around Bobby and lifts him off of the ground. "We had to walk those kids to their teacher's house so we could question them and find out all of the information about where and when we are in time and space. I hope we didn't scare you too bad."

"Speaking of being scared out of our minds," I begin with all thoughts of guilt leaving my conscious thoughts, "what's the big idea of jumping out of that tree on top of us? And the tapping, were you trying to give us heart attacks or something?"

"Sorry about that, Billy," Bobby says, though the delight in his voice tells me that he wasn't really sorry at all. "The wood tapping. It was too dramatic, no? I heard that too when I came here. There are a lot of woodpeckers in this grove of trees. They are searching for insects to eat and sounding out a warning to predators at the same time. The sound does bounce around in here, though, and freaks you out. Happens to the best of us."

"But, now that I know the two of you are okay, I have to admit that I really wasn't scared at all. I have enjoyed getting the chance to explore this place by myself. I even found a pear tree in that direction that is covered with ripe fruit, which tells me this is probably late summer to early fall. I also found a tree that is the perfect size to make a fort. With that one, no one can find us unless we want to be found." Bobby lifts his right arm to point in the direction of the pear tree, then swings his arm in another direction to indicate the other tree as well.

"I wasn't scared, either," Joanne insists stubbornly. "It will take more than you to scare me."

"That's not true," Bobby says as his lawyer persona takes over. "I saw you nearly leap out of your skin."

"Uh-huh," Joanne responds, warning how he should be scared for his life right now.

"Uh-huh," Bobby chimes back.

"Come on, you two," I begin, just a little more than merely irritated. "We have better things to worry about than who was scared and the degree to which that fear encompassed them." See, I often use big words and complex language patterns when I am trying to avoid subjects that I would much rather avoid.

"You only say that because we all know who was really scared," Joanne teases.

"Billy's right, though," Bobby defends. "Tell me what you found out."

"Well," I begin. "This is the colonial period, and England still has control over the thirteen colonies that would form the United States of America. The rebellion has begun, and the kids that we met were the children of in the tories."

"What's a tory?" Bobby asks.

"A tory is a political party consisting mainly of settlers who remain loyal to the English crown," Joanne adds. "They are also known as Loyalists in many parts of the country."

"So the historical event probably has something to do with the American Revolution," Bobby guesses. "What side were those kids on, or did they have a side?"

"They seemed to be a little mixed on where they stood on the issue," I say. "The older boy is named Jacob. He is probably a few years older than me. He seemed to side in favor of the British. The girl, on the other hand…."

"How old was she?" Bobby asks. He always takes issue with everybody being older than him.

"My guess is she was somewhere between nine and eleven," I explain without emphasizing the age difference. "She takes pride in being an American. I don't know about the mother, but the father was definitely a Loyalist."

"You even met their parents?" Bobby asks, a little annoyed at us having left out that part of the story.

"No," Joanne corrects. "We didn't have time, but we did talk about them. We have been invited to meet them. In fact, we have even been asked to stay with them until our parents are located."

"Huh? Your parents? That wasn't part of the story," Bobby reminds us.

"Joanne changed the story because she realized that they knew this area better than us, and there was a good chance of being caught in a lie," I say, knowing Bobby will see sense in this explanation. "I thought it was a good story, so I kinda' went along with her. And, as far as staying the night goes, we'll only do it if you agree to come with us."

"What? Do they know about me? Why is that?" Bobby asks, seeming a little confused.

"We told them you were our parents' servant and that we were going to set you free. We said that you ran off after the attack to find our parents. I'm sure that, if you want, we can say that you have come back, and they might let you stay with them," Joanne explains.

"Attack? Servant?" Bobby really sounds confused even though we have explained everything to him. "I told you I wasn't sure if I liked this story. You guys go ahead and spend the night. As long as I'm in no danger of being hunted down, I would just as soon stay here with my running water, my fruit trees, and my homemade fortress than begin serving you and your new friends. My parents didn't raise me up to be nobody's slave!" His tone gets heavier, and we have a hard time understanding whether or not he is still joking.

"Please don't be mad. If it is going to upset you, we just won't stay with them," I say, determined not to let this – or anything else for that matter – come between our friendship.

"Yes. I think we all should stick together. I think it's for the best. One for all and all for one." Well, she almost got it. Joanne is starting to sound like one of the three musketeers. Quite a scary thought, really.

"I'm not mad," Bobby explains. "I think that I am a bigger man than that. You need to stay with them. Talk to the adults and figure out what is going down. The sooner we can find out what will happen, the sooner we can get out of this place. Although I am starting to like it here more and more. Heck, by the time y'all are ready to go, I might have decided to stay in this paradise. HAH, HAH!"

"Okay," I agree. "If you think it's a good idea. One of us will try to sneak out tonight to let you know what we learn. If we can't sneak out, we will see you tomorrow when the kids go back to school. They invited us to go with them, but we'll skip that and come here to see you." I look to Joanne for support, but she has a concerned look on her face as she gazes at Bobby.

Bobby, meanwhile, turns his face in my direction. "Bad idea. I've been thinking about that, and since those two were talking about their new teacher and their Uncle Nathan, when we arrived, I think there is a good chance that he has something to do with the historical event. Or maybe the other teacher. Either that or maybe they know something about it. If you can't sneak out, don't worry about it, but definitely go to school with those kids. Just listen and learn what you can from them and the adults. Let me know what you find out when you can." He leans back against the tree and props his right foot on a root that is protruding from the ground. "I'll be fine."

"We will, and we'll be back every chance we get," Joanne promises. With that, she turns her head toward me and nods. "We'll find out everything we can."

"Just don't hog all of the fun. If you do, I might go back without you," Bobby threatens with a big smile creeping across his face. "Don't forget that I will have the Double-D here with me."

Chapter 5
Whose Side Are You On Anyway?
Or Let The Adventure Begin!

On the way back to Ms. Gilbert's home, or maybe it is a schoolhouse, Joanne and I walk, pretty much all of the way, in silence. The quiet feels good at first, and I think Joanne might have been simply enjoying the lack of noise we found in this time period. Although, of course, this century is not noisy compared to the twenty-first century, there is definitely a tense feeling here – much like a rubber band being pulled beyond its limits, ready to break any second now – with the talk of Patriots versus Tories and who's on whose side and even the talk of a spy. It's pretty much more than I bargained for.

Then, it starts to get annoying; the silence, that is. It is like I have to make a conscious effort not to say anything that might break the silence or an unwritten rule might be broken. I even try to think of something to get my mind off of how quiet it is becoming, but all I can think about is Joanne and what she is thinking about.

I look at her and see her blue eyes staring at the horizon, oblivious to my being by her side or even of my existence. I can tell that she is deep in thought, so I simply walk beside her in silence and wonder what she is thinking.

Finally, after it has become completely unbearable, I have to ask. "Joanne, Watcha thinkin' 'bout?" Oh, the charm of my word-play. No reply. "Joanne?" I say with a little more volume and intensity.

"Huh," she says at last. "What did you say?"

Feeling guilty for breaking that beautiful silence and a little ridiculous for not having my clever banter heard the first time, I repeat, "I said, watcha thinkin' 'bout?"

Joanne looks at me, then back into the distance ahead of us, and her eyes seem to glaze over as she speaks. "I'm wondering what historical event we are searching for and if we have enough time to find it. I mean, really, we can have already missed it completely since we don't even know what we are looking for or where to look. Maybe we are just spinning our wheels by sticking around." I can't tell if the tone in her voice is coming from homesickness or fear. Maybe I am feeling both of these emotions with her, but I am too afraid to admit it. Perhaps.

After Joanne says what she feels, I don't know what to say, so we both just continue our walk in silence. Even though I feel that Bobby is getting way too excited about this detective work to ever want to go back home, I am beginning to get deep anxiety in my insides, and I feel that something is going to go wrong. So I decide Joanne needs to know where I am on the subject of returning to our era.

"You know, Jo," I begin. "We can just   "

"She did it. I thought it might be the case. Ms. Gilbert let us go home early, and we don't even have to come back this afternoon." Jacob and Elizabeth are running at us, suddenly screaming at the top of their lungs. I figure this talk will just have to wait.

When Jacob and Elizabeth run upon us, I ask,

"How did you know where to look to find us?"

"We... We...." Elizabeth tries, but she is obviously too out of breath to finish.

"We didn't come looking for you," Jacob finishes where his sister cannot. "We knew you would return to Ms. Gilbert's house, so we have been waiting on the front stoop for you."

In astonishment, I look up to see the house not even two hundred yards from where we now stand. I really didn't think we had come this far. In fact, I thought we still had at least fifteen more minutes before we got back to the house. But, of course, I wasn't wearing my watch, and there had been a lot of walking in silence. It is not only possible for us to reach the house as fast as we did, but it is also a fact. Here we are.

"Can you speak some more, Billy?" Elizabeth asks. "The tone of your voice and the accent sound quite humorous to me."

"Elizabeth, don't tease. People from different regions don't always sound the same as us," Jacob begins. Then turning to address Joanne, he says, "Let us go to my father's house. There we can get some food and a change of clothes for you both. It is horrible the attackers came at night. It looks like they left you nothing to wear outside your night clothes."

At this, I turn to Joanne, and we exchange a slight smile. It is true. Each of us has on a pullover T-shirt that, to Jacob and Elizabeth, must look a lot like a nightshirt. Joanne doesn't have on a fancy dress like Elizabeth, either. For a girl to wear pants in this time period must have been very unthinkable. Even a woman that works in the fields or in a barn probably wears a dress to do her chores.

The only thing that I can't figure out is why they haven't asked about our clothes before now. I decide that they had talked about them after we had gone and either decided we were too poor to have clothes like theirs or our attackers really just wanted our parents and our outfits. And since they didn't want to insult us by assuming that we were poor, they assumed we lost our clothes to the thieves. I figure that dressing decently for a day or two won't do me too much harm, so I decide to go along with Jacob's plan.

"Well, come along with us," Jacob invites. "The house of my father is this way."

We begin retracing the steps that are now becoming familiar. There is no talking, so it gives me time to think. All in one morning's time, we walked to the Gilbert house, walked back to the tree, then back to the house. Now we are going back in the direction of the tree on our way to the house in which Jacob and Elizabeth live. That's when it occurs to me that we might be passing very close to the location of Bobby's new fort. This has me thinking of what might happen if the secret hiding place were to ever be discovered. That's when Jacob breaks the silence.

"You seem to be inside of your thoughts, Billy." "Huh. I mean, what did you say?" I reply.

"I said that you seem to be inside your thoughts," Jacob repeats. "Your thinking is not with us as your eyes appear to gaze at nothing. You are probably deep in concern regarding the safety of your parents."

"Yes, that's it. I'm deep inside of my thoughts," I say, fairly relieved that I can understand what he means. "We call that being deep in thought."

"I have noticed that your language is somewhat different than ours," Elizabeth says. "Some of your words are strange to me. For instance, when you say things like 'that's' and 'it's' and 'yeah.' I can understand what you are saying, but I am unaccustomed to this manner of speech."

"Please excuse my sister," Jacob offers, sounding almost embarrassed that his sister is not as intellectual as he is. "She is just not acquainted with different regional speech."

"Regional speech?" Joanne asks. I am sure that she is getting ready to come to the defense of her new little friend. This could really blow our cover.

"Yes. The way people from different areas will say the same thing in the same language and the speech comes out sounding completely different. It is as if they are not even speaking the same language. Listen to how the local people sound when talking to the freshly arrived British soldiers," Jacob explains.

"Well, Jacob, the reason your sister doesn't understand what we say all of the time is…." And that's when Joanne catches the glare I am sending her way and realizes what she is about to say. She changes course, and her eyes dart to the ground. "Uh, I mean, it's because she is younger, and she has never heard anyone from another, uh, region talk so differently like us." Now it is obvious that Joanne wanted to change the subject. "So, what does your father do for a living?"

"Do for a living?" Jacob questions, still baffled by Joannes' outburst and sudden change.

"What is his vocation," I intercede, trying to get things back on even ground and away from the stormy ocean I had seen heading our way.

"Oh, his occupation. He owns a shipping port," Jacob explains. He brings different goods over to the settlements from England."

At this point, Elizabeth steps between her brother and Joanne and takes over the conversation. They all stop walking as the conversation gets heated. "That is why he is so against anyone standing up to the motherland. He knows it will ruin his business if England has to stop exporting their goods to America."

"That is not the main reason, but there is some wisdom in the words that my sister so foolishly chooses to utter," Jacob says. He turns to his sister and chastises her with his foul glare. "That is his way of making money and affording the nice things you wear. We also need England to protect us from our enemies, the native people, and the French."

Now it is Elizabeth's turn to get a little irritated with her brother. "Without the throne behind us, we would have no enemies. In fact, you have heard the talk about the town. France is willing to help us rid ourselves of England; the Indian people might also be willing to help. Then, perhaps Father could import goods from all of the other European nations. Just imagine."

"You, young lady, had better learn your place. You are starting to sound like the Hale side of the family." Jacob warns. "I would swear you have been writing to Uncle Nathan. Father says he has turned many of their oldest friends against the king."

Instead of watching Jacob and Elizabeth argue, I watch Joanne. At first, I thought she would lose her cool at the 'young lady' comment, but I am relieved to find that she has become more interested in the direction that the conversation seemed to be going. In fact, she is watching the siblings argue so closely that I think, for sure, that she will fall over some of the stones in the path. But, thankfully, the walking has pretty much ceased.

It is about here that I notice that we are approaching the lone tree where we first popped into this peculiar state of affairs. I also see Bobby duck behind a large stone in the distance. Thank goodness, I don't think anyone sees him but me. Just to be on the safe side, I decide to divert everyone's attention to me.

"Jacob? Elizabeth?" I ask. "Why don't you tell us about your Uncle Nathan? Didn't you say he is on the Hale side of the family?"

Jacob begins, "Well, he is not really our uncle. He is the cousin of my father, and he is reputed to be a wonderful teacher. He is talking about taking Ms. Gilbert's place if our father allows it. He studied at Yale University and has been teaching students in Connecticut. Father invited him to come to Long Island in hopes of getting him out of that territory. You see, there are many patriots in that area, and father fears his cousin might join the forces of General Washington. We have heard rumors that he is involved in the siege of Boston, but I am sure Father would have never asked him to come here if he believed anything of that rumor. Father has had a falling out with Uncle Nathan, but seeing as he is the favorite relative of Elizabeth, he did have compassion on the man."

"He is my favorite," Elizabeth all but bursts out. "And he used to be your favorite, too, until Father turned you against him."

At this remark, Jacob simply goes dumb. I'm unsure if he is searching in his mind for a rebuttal after his sister's statement or if he is just mulling over what she said. The statement might have hit closer to home than Jacob will ever be willing to admit.

We begin walking again in silence. Then, about five minutes later, Elizabeth begins shouting. "There it is. That is the house of my father." She is referring to a large house, set off by itself. From over the hill, just past the house, one can see the tops of other homes, though none seem as big or as elegant. I feel like commenting on the fact that we have seen so few houses up to this point, but I realize that the houses would have been spread out except in the city, which we are now on the outskirts of.

And as we walk closer to the house, Elizabeth continues to fill us in on the area at about a thousand words per second. She points at the well that she had become trapped in when she was too young to remember, and she shows us a tree with a swing on it that her father planted. She also tells us that her father planted that tree so that he might later put the swing on it just for her. He is obviously a man that loves his children and listening to Elizabeth now, it is clear that he is also a man that is loved by his children.

Chapter 6
A New Family, Or Is That Your Mom?

As we walk up to the gorgeous stone house, it seems we are getting smaller. Joanne is walking in front next to the left of Jacob, and I am behind her with Elizabeth on my right.

The stones on the house are placed randomly, though it appears that every stone is exactly where it is supposed to be. And although the house is enormous, it has class and character, unlike the mansions of the super-rich and famous homes that you see in twenty-first century Hollywood. It also can't be compared to the high- rise hotels and office buildings that cover the Long Island landscape of my time.

The trim on the house is painted yellow, and the house has lattice work around the windows on the second story of the structure. I want to ask if they have a swimming pool out back, but I am pretty sure I already know the answer. 'What's a swimming pool?'

As I am observing the outside of this mini-castle with my eyes, a beautiful woman walks by one of the windows and looks down at us. Before she walks away, I see that she has on a light blue dress with white trim, and her hair is put back in a bun. The skin on her face seems as smooth and white as milk, and her teeth sparkle as she smiles at us.

"Is that your, mom?" I ask, not paying attention if I am addressing Jacob or Elizabeth. "She is very pretty."

"No," replies Elizabeth. "That is the woman my father pays to clean the house. If it would please you, I could introduce you. She is very nice."

"Oh, I would really like to meet...." I start, but then Joanne interrupts my thought.

"We would love to meet the woman that cleans your house, but we would really rather meet your parents," she says. "Are they home?" Then she turns to me and gives me a glare that says, 'don't blow this opportunity.'

As if in response to Joanne's question, another woman comes out of the house. Though I don't think she is as pretty as the first woman, this new one has a striking look. She seems to be a powerful woman even though her size is no bigger than Jacob's. She has light brown hair, like Jacob's, and her dress is a lot like Elizabeth's. Both dresses have layers of cloth on the skirt, though the tightness around the waist of the elder of the two seems to be a little forced. Also, like Elizabeth's dress, you can't see the shoes, though I am sure she has them on her feet.

"Welcome home, children. Who are your friends?" the woman asks.

"These are some acquaintances we met on our way to school today, mother," Jacob starts. "They have quite a story to tell."

I am nervous that Jacob uses the word story, which could imply we are not telling the truth. I feel better when Elizabeth takes over, as she does not have the patience of Jacob. "They have come from Virginia with their parents, who were taken away by some bandits, probably redcoats, and now they are looking for a place to stay. Can we keep them, mother? Please."

Of course, we will take them in and help in any way we can, but please don't let your father hear you use the term 'redcoats.' You know how he feels about that." Then, turning her attention to me, she asks, "Please, young children. Tell me your names."

I am ready to introduce myself and Joanne if she lets me when Elizabeth goes on, "Their names are Joanne and Billy, and they...."

Elizabeth is cut off sharply by her mother.

"Elizabeth, I would really prefer hearing from those with whom I have inquired. Please let me hear from them if you would be so polite. I'm sorry, children, go on."

"Well," I start, "my name is Billy Mac, though you can call me Billy, and this is my sister, Joanne. Elizabeth was doing a good job of telling you our story. You see, my parents were bringing us up here to Long Island when we were ambushed on the way. My sister and I were away from the camp then, so we were not taken. I am sure they will be released soon, so we can go back to them."

"Is Elizabeth correct when she suggested that the British soldiers took them?" the woman inquires.

"We really don't know who took them," I explain, in my best 'I-am-not-telling-a-lie' way. "All we really know is that they were gone when we returned. There were a lot of horse imprints in the ground, and the camp had been ransacked."

"Did anyone escape besides yourselves?" the mother continues to question. I am afraid, at this point, that our story might be falling apart.

"They had a slave-child with them," Jacob tells. "But he escaped when they discovered the others were taken. Billy thinks that he might return when the initial fear leaves him. I, however, think we might be able to help them locate their servant."

When Jacob says this, I begin to worry about Bobby's safety. "Why do you say this, Jacob? Have you seen him?" I ask, trying to distract the others. "He said he was going to look for the others. We trust he will return."

"How could I have seen him? I have been with you the whole time, have I not?"

This is true. We left Jacob and Elizabeth at their teacher's house, visited with Bobby, then came back to where we left them. I still wanted to get everybody off of the subject of Bobby. But that wasn't to be. Their mother continues with her questioning once again. "Tell me about your servant. Is he indentured to you, paying off a debt to your family, or is he an African? They are common in Virginia, or so I hear."

Neither, mother," Elizabeth cuts in again. "He is a brown-skinned one. I hope we can find him. I have only seen one other."

"Sister, that means he has come from Africa," Jacob chimes in as if his sister knows nothing. "Have you not been doing your studies as you should?"

"I have," Elizabeth says defensively. "But I have not studied much about the African continent, Yet."

"They are not only on the African continent. They are here, as well. This is something that you should know," Jacob says sneakily.

"Well, you children are certainly welcome to stay with us until your parents are located," the woman says. "My husband is a powerful man in this community, and if anyone can locate your servant, I am sure he will be able to do so."

"Thank you for your concern and hospitality, Mrs..." Joanne begins, and it dawns on me that we don't know their last names or what to call the mom.

Mrs. Yardshire," the woman completes. Then, turning to face Joanne, she continues, "So tell me, Joanne. What is bringing you to Long Island, all the way from Virginia?"

Finally, questions were directed towards Joanne and not me. I was hoping to answer this one, but surely Joanne remembers the answer that I gave to Jacob earlier this morning.

CHAPTER 7
THE DREAM

I am walking through a tunnel, but I remain unsure of where the tunnel leads. For that matter, I'm not sure where the tunnel begins. To the best of my recollection, I don't remember climbing into a tunnel. I also don't know if I am the type of person who is brave enough to climb into a strange tunnel by myself, but here I am.

The ground is covered in dense fog, so I cannot see what I am walking on. The circular, cement walls of the tunnel I am walking through have now given way to a square-shaped walkway that appears to be made of wood. The ground, however, doesn't feel hard enough to be made of wood, It definitely isn't concrete anymore, and steel is out of the question. I guess the flooring is soft dirt, but there is something about this thought that gives me the creeps.

I look as far as I can see in front of me, hoping that I might be able to get some idea as to where it is I am going. Though the tunnel is not pitch-black, it is dark enough to keep me from seeing anything too far away. I guess I can see 25 feet in front of me. The tunnel I am in is also winding so that, even if it were possible for me to

see far down the walkway, the walls of the tunnel would still keep me from seeing too far ahead.

Still not knowing where I am going, I decide to see where I am coming from, so I turn back to look. I know I have been walking, though I don't know for how long, and I know I have been on only one path. The puzzling thing is that now, behind me, there are many different paths. I never noticed the tunnel opening up as I walked through, but apparently, the path I am on has opened up to a juncture, a place where many pathways all come together.

When I attempt to count the tunnels that lead to this particular place, I keep seeing another tunnel, then another one, and another. All of these tunnels are new. They had not been here before, or maybe they were just out of my sight. But here they are.

I keep turning my body to face the new tunnel, and I keep turning to face the next one, and then the next one, until I am convinced I have turned all of the ways around in a half circle. But, now that I am perhaps facing the original direction that I walked in earlier, I notice that there isn't a solitary tunnel in front of me anymore, but rather many tunnels. Somehow, I have walked into a junction of tunnels to my rear and tunnels in front of me. I am in the center of tunnel entrances, or so it appears.

Not knowing where I am going or where I have come from, I decide to stop trying to find a particular path and just pick one and go in that direction. I walk to the entrance nearest me only to discover a sign blocking the opening. It reads:

EXIT;

One Way;

Do Not Enter!

I turn away from that opening, finally deciding that this must be the tunnel that I came out of in the first place. I pick the opening to the pathway just opposite the one with the sign, but when I get to this entrance, another sign is blocking the way:

EXIT;

One Way;

Do Not Enter!

Not the right doorway. I choose to go to the pathway directly to the right of the second one I chose. But again:

EXIT;

One Way;

Do Not Enter!

Now I feel my heart beat faster as I begin to panic. I begin running from one path to the next, hoping to find one that is not an exit. Everyone is marked with a sign, and they all read:

EXIT;

One Way;

Do Not Enter!

Finally, a thought occurs to me. Return to the middle of the circle of paths because that is where I belong. I don't know why I think that I belong there, but a gut feeling tells me I do, and that is where I need to go. Once I move back to the center of the circle of pathways,

I sit on the fog-covered floor, not concerned with the direction I am facing or where I have already been. I am exhausted and trapped, but this is where I choose to be.

After sitting, I notice that I can brush the dense fog away from certain areas by waving my hand. Now it is possible to see what I have been walking on. It is dirt. But not just plain dirt. It is old dirt. Dirt that has been in the same place for a long time, maybe even eons or eons upon eons. Dirt that has not seen the light of day in just as many years. Old and rotting compost.

I brush away a layer of old dirt to see what is underneath. It is surprising how easily and quickly the dirt moves to reveal a flat piece of stone with grooves chiseled into it. As I brush away more dirt from the stone, I realize that the grooves in the stone form letters, and I continue until I can read the words.

'Here Lies Jacob Yardshire,' the stone reads.

In a panic, I dust away another area of the soft dirt, not knowing why I don't just get away from the area as fast as I can. The second area of dirt has another stone with letters on it. These letters reveal the words, 'Here lies Elizabeth Yardshire.'

This is awful. Apparently, all of this soft dirt I have been trodding upon is a graveyard. I stand and look and look around me, and I see more stones with more

writings. I see stones upon stones as far as the eye can see. I am in the middle of a cemetery with no end. I have been walking on graves; worse, I know the people whose names are written on the gravestones.

I scream and am suddenly thrust up in the air toward who knows what. I sit up in bed, still screaming, and realize I am back in the bedroom that belongs to the Yardshires.

The door bursts open, and in runs Joanne. "What's the matter," she asks in a voice that is not a whisper, not loud enough to awaken the entire household as if they are not awake already. I continue screaming, but not quite as loud a scream as what I am hearing in my head, and I don't know why I could not stop. I don't know if I should be held like an infant or just swatted on the head for my cowardice.

Just as I am on the verge of getting myself back in control, Mrs. Yardshire runs inside, followed by Jacob and Elizabeth. The sight of Yardshire just brings back the memory of the dream, and I continue to scream, trying to decide how to stop the nightmare from coming to fruition.

At last, Mrs. Yardshire holds me and places my head on her shoulder, and this does help me to get myself under control. I stop screaming, but I am still breathing heavily.

"I know," Mrs. Yardshire comforts. "You have been through so much. It is no wonder you have had a bad dream, probably having to do with your parents." After saying that, she turns her head to the others in the room. "All of you need to leave. Billy will be just fine."

Jacob and Elizabeth leave the room, but Joanne stays behind to help.

"You go, too, dear," Mrs. Yardshire says. "Leave your brother with me. He will be better with some room to breathe."

Joanne leaves reluctantly, and the Yardshire matriarch turns my face toward hers. "Hear me well, child. You might find it helpful to tell me of the dream that frightened you so very terribly."

I still haven't processed the dream fully, so I am afraid to tell someone from this century anything I do not completely understand myself. I especially don't want to tell Mrs. Yardshire that I dreamed I was walking on the graves of her children. She might think I am sick in the head or something like that. Maybe I am.

"I saw my parents being taken away by some soldiers," I whisper, knowing that the truth is impossible. "I think they had red uniforms. I cannot remember any more than that. I am sorry."

"You do not need to worry about any of that right now," she continues. "I just want you to lay your head back down and try to sleep for a little while longer. The bad dream will fade out of your head. My husband will be home soon and will be interested to hear more of your story. The one about you and your sister."

She leaves the room, and I do as I'm told. Soon enough, I am back in the gentle arms of slumber. No dream, good or bad, comes to me on this night. It has to be the soundest sleep I have ever had in my life.

CHAPTER 8
UNCLE WHO?

When I wake up again, much earlier than I want to due to the previous night's dream, I am lying in bed, not in some goofy tunnel. Coming up into my room from downstairs, and I guess it lingers throughout the house, is a smell that makes my mouth water and my stomach grumble.

I can't tell what it is yet, but I can tell that I will enjoy eating this morning. After all that has happened to my little group, I am having a hard time remembering when I ate last. My mind says it was the last morning, which will have been this afternoon in my time, but my stomach argues that it has been a few days. I guess this feeling must be something like jet lag on steroids.

Getting out of bed, I follow my nose out into the hallway and down the stairs. Of course, I am brushing my hair with my hands the entire way to make it look halfway straight. After all, I will probably be seeing Joanne at breakfast, and I don't want her to think that I woke up with a messy head of hair.

Upon reaching the bottom of the stairs, I take notice of my surroundings. The walls in the house are covered with straight wooden planks that have been painted white, and the doorways and trim are adorned with a fine wood finish. I look to my right, where my nose is telling me to go, and I start walking down another hallway that leads to the kitchen.

Lo and behold, I find the beautiful girl who smiled at me from the upstairs window here, cooking and serving breakfast. She is wearing a black dress that has white lace lining the bottom of the skirt as if to say, these shoes are not for your eyes. It seems that she is not just the cleaning lady; she is also the cook – and quite a good one at that.

While I stand in the entrance to the kitchen, gawking at the heavenly form before me, I don't notice the steps walking up behind me. Then I hear, "Mm-hmn."

Someone is behind me, watching me as I stare at this woman in the kitchen. That's okay. I am not afraid of being watched. I am doing nothing wrong except looking on as someone is serving breakfast. This would only scare me if it happened to be...

"What are you looking at?" Joanne's voice asks. The voice that normally turns my heart to butter with its warmth and kindness now sounds like an icy voice from the northern polar cap.

"Uh," I stammer. "The smell of good cooking brought me down here. I was hoping you would already be here."

"Yes," Joanne says with her voice a little less frosty. "The smell brought me down here too, but my knees didn't buckle at the kitchen doorway."

"Huh?" I ask, trying to sound unaffected by the woman in front of the girl behind me or me. "I don't know why I stopped in the doorway. My mind just went blank. Maybe I had some kind of seizure."

"Makes no never-mind to me," Joanne says, her voice as icy as it was when she first walked up. "As far as I'm concerned, you can go into these seizures anytime you feel inclined to do so."

Just in time, Mrs. Yardshire walks into the square room and rings a little brass bell that is on the counter. She is wearing a long, brown gown that goes all the way to the floor. In the words of the twenty-first century, she doesn't have a hair out of place. I assume the bell is meant to indicate to the rest of the family that it is now time to come to the dining room for the morning meal. My thoughts are, 'saved by the bell.'

The lady of the household speaks. "Good morning, children. Louise, have you met our lovely houseguests yet? This is Joanne Mac and her brother Billy Mac."

At this introduction, I smile, though I want to laugh hysterically. The woman of the household has picked up on my nickname and mistaken it for my last name. And, since Joanne and I are supposed to be siblings, she has assumed that my sister's last name is the same as mine. 'Mac.'

"I am very happy to meet you," the young woman says with a slight but distinct accent that I think is French, but I cannot be certain. She flashes me one of the warmest, most sincere smiles that I can imagine, and then she stands up straight and bends her knees a tiny bit, making her body go lower a few inches before she lifts herself up again.

Joanne whispers in my ear, "That's called a curtsy. You must nod your head forward to indicate you are bowing back to her."

"Huh," I say, taken aback for a second. Then grasping the meaning, I do what I have seen done by actors on some of my favorite old western shows. I tilt my head forward, bringing my right hand up as if to touch the rim of my cowboy hat. I am on the verge of saying, "Howdy, ma'am. Nice to make your acquaintance", when Joanne kicks the back of my shoe to indicate I should stop before I go overboard.

"John has gone to town with Jacob and Elizabeth. You fell asleep early and slept through dinner," Mrs.

Yardshire states, facing Joanne and me as she speaks. "They should be back soon." Then, turning to face Louise, she inquires, "Is the food almost ready? I am sure our young houseguests are very hungry."

That last statement is the understatement of the year. I know I am starving, and I suspect Joanne is, as well. As I nod my head vigorously, Louise says, "Oui, madam, s'il vous plait," as she turns and rushes to get the food on the table.

"Aren't the others going to eat this meal with us?" I ask. I am having a hard time imagining that we will eat before the others, but I am not upset. Hunger is starting to set in, making it hard for me to think.

"Billy, you both slept in. John and the children have already had their morning meal, and they have been gone for an hour," Mrs. Yardshire says, turning from Joanne to me. After this, she turns and leaves the room.

During breakfast, when I suspect no one is looking, I try to fold pieces of food into my napkin. I also notice that Joanne is doing the same thing. I guess we are both thinking of Bobby, knowing that he is going to need something more to eat than a bunch of pears.

When Louise walks in to take our plates, I realize that having two fine napkins disappear from the table will not go unnoticed. I stand to face her and say, "Joanne and I are going to go in search of our parents. If we find them, they will be hungry. Can we take some food with us to feed them if we can find them?"

"Oui, I mean, yes, of course," she begins, letting her French slip out while talking to us. "Take the food and bring your families back here if you can find them. I will have more food that I can feed them. Now, go, go. Mrs. Yardshire will not like that you went by yourselves, so you must hurry. I will let her know where you have gone."

So, Joanne and I leave the house and head back in the direction where we last saw Bobby. It is a good walk, and I agree to carry the food items that we have with us. We are both glad to be getting back to our friend.

When we arrive at the small grove of trees, Bobby once again jumps out of a tree to greet us, but this time he does not land on top of me. He begins sniffing the air and says, "What have you brought? It smells delicious." He takes the food that I give him and sits on the ground to begin eating. He barely says a word between bites. I don't think he wants to tell us that he is hungry, and we don't need to ask. The hunger shows in the speed at which he devours his food.

After Bobby has eaten, the three of us lie down under the trees and listen to the woodpecker's peck out their warnings. The pecking noises aren't nearly as loud or pervasive as they were yesterday. Bobby has been with them all day, and I guess they are used to having company under the trees.

"So you have made new friends that can help you find out what it is you need to know about this time period," Bobby states. "What have you learned so far?"

"Well," I begin, "the kids have a teacher who is about to quit teaching them."

"Yes," Joanne continues, "and their uncle Nathan is coming to make sure their education continues—"

Joanne interrupts, "I don't know if he plans to teach them himself or just make sure their next teacher is a proficient educator. In any case, that is all we know so far. I know we can't stay here much longer, but once we know anything, we will come back out to get you so that you can watch history being made with us."

"I think what Joanne is trying to say is that we have to get back," I begin as if it is my turn to talk. "We will get by every chance we can to keep you updated and feed you some yummy food."

Joanne and I leave, heading back to the house. On the way back, we discuss what we think is going on in this time period. We discuss what the historical event might be, and we even talk about the algebra test we have to take next Friday when we return to the twenty-first century.

CHAPTER 9
THE CONFLICT

When we arrive back at the house, it is late in the morning, and nobody appears to be home. The door isn't locked, so we let ourselves in, and that is when we hear somebody moving around upstairs. "That is probably Louise," Joanne states as if she knows what she is talking about... I am about to tell her that there is a fifty-fifty chance it is Mrs. Yardshire. But before I can say anything, I am saved from being wrong again when the Lady of the House comes out of her study to greet us.

"There you are," she exclaims, raising her arms in the air and coming to stand in front of us. "I knew you had gone, but I was not sure at what time you were going to return. Were you able to locate your parents?"

"Not yet," I say. I am beginning to get into this pretending thing. "I am still sure they will show up. The soldiers may have taken them. So they will probably be released. We just do not know."

"I am sure that you are correct," she goes on. "John and the kids are telling others to be on the lookout for them, and if they are found, the people of this community will assist in any way they can."

She pauses and glances at the front door of the house. "Speaking of John and the kids, I think I can hear them walking up the porch steps this very instant."

The door to the house swings open, and a big man is standing in the doorway. Behind him, to the right, is Jacob and to the left is Elizabeth.

Mrs. Yardshire walks to the front door to greet her husband. As he walks through the door, I notice that he is not fat or round in the sense that I might call someone big in my own century, but he is muscular and, well, just big. The best I can do to describe him is to compare him to a linebacker for a professional football team. I get the impression that this man does not just own the loading dock but also helps load and unload the cargo. His hair is blond like that of Elizabeth, and he has a neatly kept blond beard, not gruff like his size might suggest.

He walks into the house with Jacob and Elizabeth trailing behind and goes straight to Joanne. She is taller than me but looks like a midget next to him. Then the big man does the unexpected. He picks Joanne up off the floor and begins to spin her around. "You must be Joanne," he bellows. "It is so good to finally get a chance to meet you. I have heard many good things about you."

When Joanne is dizzy and maybe a little sick, Mr. Yardshire sets her down and balances her so that she doesn't tip over. Then he walks to where I am standing, picks me up effortlessly, and performs the same twirling motion that I witnessed him do to Joanne. "And you, too, little Billy. You are both a welcome addition to our household."

I find the whole situation just a little bit embarrassing. Here is this man that we have never met before, and he is treating us like his long-lost cousins. It is a little nice, and no formal introductions are necessary, but Mrs. Yardshire begins the introduction process.

"Yes, dearest. These are the children I told you about. Little Billy and Joanne Mac. They have the most wonderful manners, and I hope they will always feel welcome in our house."

After the introductions are behind us and the embarrassment of being called 'Little Billy' has simmered down just a hair, we are all ready to sit down to eat. Mr. Yardshire must have filled in on our make-believe history before we met him because he doesn't even ask about our parents.

The meal itself is eaten with very little talk, as well. Occasionally, Joanne or I are asked about our families during the meal, but these questions are easy to dodge because everyone assumes that we are both still in shock from what we have been through. If they only knew the half of it.

I don't know, for sure, how many portions of the meal I ate, but I am shocked that a small-framed body like mine can hold as much as it does. Every time my plate looks like it is getting empty, Louise shows up with more and fills it up again.

Finally, I get to the point where the thought of eating anything else will probably make me puke, and this is definitely something that I do not want to do in front of Joanne, pretend sister or not. Who knows. If I don't puke, she might start liking me if she can ever get over being angry at me for staring at Louise in the kitchen.

When I think things can't go any better, I discover they won't. "John," Mrs. Yarshire begins. "I talked with Nelda from up the way. She told me I should tell you there is a letter for you in town. I believe she said it was from Ned Burton down in Virginia. I just cannot imagine what he would have to say, knowing how you feel about the English and the Patriots."

"Oh, no," Mr. Yardshire responds. "I hope it is not bad news about my cousin, Nathaniel Hale. Good Lord, I hope he has not gotten into trouble on his trip. This Patriot group is growing. With his attitude, he might get himself into trouble."

"Dear, you cannot watch after every step he takes," she continues. "I think you did the right thing in trying to keep him safe by giving him this opportunity to teach in Long Island. You only did that to keep him from being further influenced by that Patriot bunch."

At this point, I realize that 'Uncle Nathan' is Nathan Hale, and there is something about that name that rings a bell. I'm not sure what it is, but I am sure that he has something to do with the historical event we are so desperately trying to find.

Mr. Yardshire stands and hits his large fist on the table, making everything shake. I quickly grab my glass before it falls over, making a mess on the tablecloth. "Ah, those troublemakers," he says in a loud voice. "If I find out that Nathaniel has gotten further involved with them, I don't know what I will do. I heard a rumor in town that he might have had something to do with the Boston siege when the Patriots kept the British soldiers bottled up on the peninsula for two months. They are starting to call that incident the Battle of Bunker Hill. If he does any rabble-rousing around here, I might just hang him, myself... I am bringing him here, and I can send him back wrapped in a blanket."

"Maybe we should stop talking about this in front of the children," Mrs. Yardshire suggests. "After all, he is your cousin, and we do not want them to think bad of him."

I feel like shouting, 'No, keep talking about it,' but I know this isn't the time or the place for me to get involved, and, as expected, the taking gets quieter and quieter until no words can be heard.

CHAPTER 10
A SPY AMONG US

After prayers are said and everyone is in bed, I am lying here, still awake, trying to figure out why we are in this time period. Before going to bed, I get the opportunity to speak to Joanne in the hallway. She says she doesn't know what might happen with Uncle Nathan. I decide it is a good time to sneak out to see Bobby and get his take on the situation. The only question that remains is whether I am alert enough to figure out a way out of this house without being noticed. Thank goodness that everyone chooses to go to bed quite early. It is only about ten o'clock, and everyone in the house is fast asleep... everyone, but me.

I take my backpack, with all of the notes from our adventure, out from under my bed. Then I decide that I don't need it since it will be too dark to write, so I put it back. The window seems the quickest and quietest way out, so I climb onto the slanting roof.

There is a tree close to Joanne's window. So, I silently move in that direction along the eaves. The tree is just out of my reach, but I figure I can make it if I jump. I back up practically to the window of Joanne's room, and I just get my legs ready to jump when I hear a noise from the tree. I try to halt so fast that I am lucky my legs don't just split in half. This split second of indecision causes me to fall over, head first, and roll to the end of the roof. As I tumble over, I grab what I can and hold on.

I am dangling ten feet above the ground with nothing underneath me but the hard ground. Hanging there, on the end of the roof, I realize how fortunate I am that I didn't fall forward and land on my head. I let go of the house and fall to the ground, landing on my feet. The jolt is numbing to my knees, but I will recover.

As I stand straight, I hear the noise at the top of the tree that caused the problem, though it did get me down faster. It is an owl, probably laughing at the misery it has caused me on this night. And as I walk to Bobby's fort, I realize I could have just used the front door. These people don't have burglar alarms. Heck, they don't even lock their doors.

When I reach the trees that Bobby uses as his home away from home, I look around very carefully, especially up in the trees. I really don't want him to jump down and scare me again.

"Bobby," I whisper. "Where are you?"

"Right behind you," he responds loudly in my right ear.

Startled again, I spin around as fast as I can, tripping over my feet and falling to the ground at Bobby's feet. Somehow, even with my super-alert settings on, he has managed to sneak up behind me and scare me half to death once again. This is beginning to get on my nerves.

"Don't do that," I shout as I take the hand he offers to help me up. "You know, people can hear my screams from miles away."

But it is no use. Bobby laughs so hard that he rolls around and falls to the ground. I think I can make out him saying, 'then don't scream,' in between the gales of laughter.

"Stop it. Get up," I insist. "Have you no dignity?" I wanted to ask him to at least leave me with a little bit of dignity. "Listen up. Here's what we have learned so far."

After Bobby manages to stop laughing, I can tell him about that day's happenings. He is particularly interested in the political views of Elizabeth since she is the only person in the Yardshire family who favors the upcoming revolution. When I get to the part about what is said at dinner and the conversation we hear from the top of the stairs, he gets extremely quiet.

Finally, after about a minute of deep thought when the story is complete, he starts talking, "I think the name 'Hale' is starting to ring a bell, but I cannot quite put my finger on what he does. Much of what seems to be happening is centered around him."

Then, Bobby bows his head as if he needs to think more about what I have told him.

I am excited to learn that I am not the only one who thinks the historical event involves Mr. Hale, but we have to find out how.

Bobby's head remains bowed down as he says, "Did you happen to catch his first name. Maybe that will help us remember what he does."

"Yes," I say, feeling embarrassed that I had not told him the name. The first name is what puts the puzzle pieces together. "His name is Nathaniel... Nathan Hale."

"And he is sent into the enemy territory by George Washington to spy on the British troops," Bobby begins slowly. As he continues, his speech gets faster, and his head slowly begins to rise.

"He is captured before delivering any information to the Patriots, and he is hanged. Come on, Billy. Surely you remember his famous speech."

"The only regret I have is...." Bobby begins, as I join him in the familiar speech that is said to have inspired many to join the revolution, "that I have but one life to lose for my country."

Chapter 11
Guilty Of Being A Patriot

I awake with a start at what sounds like a slamming door. Looking out of the window, I decide that it must be about 9:00 in the morning, and I really do not feel like getting up just yet. The bed in this room is so comfortable that all I really want to do is lay here all day.

And next comes the yelling. I can't make out what is being said, and I am not entirely sure I want to. The voice that I am hearing, without a doubt, belongs to Mr. Yardshire. I am worried that Joanne and I might be suspected of being spies. Jacob and Elizabeth's father might have gone out this morning and checked up on the story that we have been telling him. If he suspects that we have been lying to him all along, he might associate our arrival with that of Nathan Hale. And knowing that Nathan will soon be tried and hanged for being a spy really makes me fear for my own life. The Tories in this area could start a spy hunt, much like a witch hunt, where anybody new to the area or just a tad bit different might be tried and hanged.

But where does it begin? That is the question that Bobby and I were asking ourselves after we discovered who Mr. Hale really is. How does he get captured? Is

Benedict Arnold, the famous officer in the American army who turns out to be a spy, already at work… spying on the Patriots? The history books from school don't mention these details. Nobody ever thinks that this information will ever be needed as badly as we need it now.

Then I hear a faint knock on the door. "Who is it?" I whisper just loud enough to be heard.

"It's me, Joanne. Open the door. You have to hear this."

I quickly throw on my jeans and run to the door. I decide to give Joanne some of her own words. I open the door a crack and whisper back, "What are you doing at my bedroom door? Have you no manners?!"

"That was different," Joanne explains. "Now let me in before I have to break down the door."

As I open the door, I notice that Joanne is wearing a fancy dress, one very similar to the one Elizabeth was wearing yesterday. She comes into the room and begins her explanation.

"We need to hear what is being said downstairs. I'm not sure, but I have a feeling it has something to do with the historical event we are searching for. The loud voice belongs to Mr. Yardshire. Listen," she instructs.

I start to fill Joanne in on what Bobby and I discovered last night, but when I try to open my mouth to speak, I am shushed and Joanne holds a finger up to her lips.

It is difficult deciphering exactly what is being said. Mr. Yardshire shouts every word so it is not hard to make out what he is saying, but Mrs. Yardshire must be right next to him. When she responds to him or makes any kind of comment at all, the sound is unheard. We have to take guesses at what she is saying. But, man, can we hear Mr. Yardshire! From the way, he is ranting and raving it is plain to see that he has a lot to say, and he seems to be afraid that no one will be able to hear him.

"He is going to get it. I cannot believe that Nathaniel would actually agree to something like this. Do you know how much trouble he is going to be in?"

There is a pause at this point in the conversation. I call it a pause, but I am pretty sure that Mrs. Yardshire is answering the question that was asked of her. After a few seconds, Mr. Yardshire continues. "I cannot. He is my cousin. The nephew of my mother. The son of my aunt. How could I do a thing like that?"

Another pause in the conversation. When Elizabeth's father begins speaking again, there is a quiver in the voice that rings from downstairs. If he hadn't been crying before, he is now.

"And to think I trusted him…! I even tried to get him out of the way of the trouble developing around us. They say he was asked by George Washington himself. I am afraid that I do not know how to save him. They will eventually find out about this no matter what we try to do."

There is the last pause before the conversation taking place downstairs ends. This pause, however, is not the same as all of the others. In this one, we are able to hear a faint female voice. The voice is also quivering and sounds upset, though it is much too faint to tell for sure. We cannot make out what she is saying.

Then we hear the familiar male voice that has been loudly ringing in our ears. He is not quite as loud, so we have to strain to hear what he is saying, but the intention seems clear. "Of course, you are correct," he begins. The officials might think that I am involved with Nathan in the planning of this entire thing, and there is no telling what they might do to me, to our family. It really is my only option."

After this last comment, we wait anxiously to hear what might be said to clarify what they are talking about, but we hear the front door creak open and then slam shut. I sneak over to the front window in my room and peek out. I remain careful not to be seen, but I don't think I have much to be worried about. The room is dark, and it is light enough outside to hide me in the darkness.

While I watch from the upstairs window Jacob comes running up to his father. I wish that I could hear what the two are saying, but I can only see them and I can't read lips. Whatever Jacob is telling him concerns me and Joanne, and it is quite obvious. He keeps pointing up to our rooms. Then, as if for no other reason but to enjoy each other's company, they both turn away from the house.

That's when Joanne grabs me. "Billy," she says. "Whatever was said downstairs sounds like the historical event that we've been trying to find. Let's stop for a moment and try to piece together what we know so far about Nathaniel Hale."

"Joanne," I say sadly as I place the conversation that we just heard into the events and revelations of last night. "Nathaniel Hale is the famous spy that Bobby and I studied in our history class last month. I believe that soon he will be captured and hanged for treason against the British crown."

"Is he the one who had the famous speech, 'I only regret that I have but one life to live for my country'?" she asks.

"One life to lose, but that's close enough," I correct. It feels pretty good to know something that Joanne doesn't already know. "Some say it didn't happen, and the truth may be lost to history… until now. What did you make of the conversation we just heard?"

"I wasn't sure, but it sounded like he was going to try to keep himself out of trouble," Joanne sounds emotional when she says this.

"I know that, but how do you think he is going to do it?" I ask. "What can he do to make himself look innocent without hurting his cousin?"

"I don't know, but it doesn't look good. Do you think he is going to–" Joanne offers weakly. She can't imagine a person giving up their family member to the enemy, and frankly, neither can I. So, it goes without saying.

"He would never…." I say, but I see absolutely no way out for John Yardshire. "Let's look at everything we know so far."

Joanne begins to speak when I stop. "We know that there are a lot of British troops in this area. Maybe it is because of the Boston revolts, but this area is teeming with them."

"Remember, they are known as the Redcoats to most of the colonies. This is because they wear bright red uniform coats," I add. I am enjoying the opportunity to interrupt her train of thought for a change. But the information is correct and appropriate.

"Right," she continues. "And the Loyalists, or Tories, don't want to break away from England, for whatever reason. I guess they are afraid of not having the safety of the English troops."

"The Patriots are the good guys. They are the colonists who are trying to win their independence from Great Britain (or England). Some of them just want to be treated like citizens. The colonists were having to pay heavy taxes and they felt they should not be taxed unless they had a representative in the Parliament, the British legislative body."

"Now," I say, "we know that Nathaniel Hale is a patriot sent by General Washington to sneak behind enemy lines to teach school."

"No," Joanne corrects. "He is going to act like he is teaching school while he spies on the British. He will then try to get anything he finds out to the other Patriots so they can know what the Redcoats are doing. What a perfect plan."

"I understand that he really is a teacher," I correct.

"He even has his degree from Yale."

"I guess I didn't know that about him. He is a teacher," Joanne agrees. "By the way, why do you think Mr. Yardshire was so upset? Did you know how he acted like he was going to slip a gasket or something?"

"Slip a gasket? He is afraid that he will get into trouble for inviting Mr. Hale here in the first place. After all, who allowed the great American spy to infiltrate behind enemy lines?" I ask.

"Mr. Yardshire," Joanne answers. "I hate to say this, but you know that he is going to turn Nathan Hale into the Redcoats to save his business, his family, and even his life." She finally gets out in the open that which we have both been fighting to believe.

"I have to tell Bobby so we can get into town and hear if he says the speech or not," I say. "After all, seeing history in action is the only reason we are still here."

Just then, there is a knock on the door. Mrs. Yardshire walks in as the door swings inward. "Good morning, Sleepyhead. I hope my husband did not awaken you. When I saw that Joanne was not in the lower part of the house, I decided that you must be visiting on this level. We have already eaten our morning meal, but yours is being warmed in the kitchen."

This takes me back for a moment. I cannot believe that I slept so long that Joanne has already been downstairs, visiting. Not only that, but she has already eaten. I guess it is understandable, though. I was up late last night talking to Bobby.

"Thank you, Mrs. Yardshire," I say, not quite knowing how to take all of this hospitality. "I am very hungry."

"Before we eat, however, I have found a change of clothes for you to put on your body," she says. "They used to belong to Jacob, but he outgrew them. They might still be a little big on you, though. The dress your sister is wearing used to belong to one of the neighbors' daughters, but she ran off to marry a young Patriot fellow down in the North Carolina territory."

As she says this, she hands me an undershirt, a plain white button-up shirt, and a pair of slacks. Along with this are a pair of socks and, what I might call, some underpants, though they had long legs that went down to my knees and had a tie-string at the top. She then picks up my clothes from the previous day and takes them away.

When the girls leave, I slip out of my night clothes – more like a very long shirt – and slip into my new clothes. I know that I need a bath, but I simply don't have time. I put my tennis shoes in my backpack, along with my notes from our adventure. I know I can return later for the rest of my things.

When I get down to the table, I have fried eggs, bacon, and hot biscuits waiting for me. I have to drink plain water for breakfast. Usually, I drink milk, but I don't care. It is nice to have a good meal before I begin what's about to be a very busy day.

Mrs. Yardshire is sitting at the table with Joanne, and she informs me that Jacob has gone off to help his father at the dock and that

Elizabeth has gone along to watch. They have asked that we come to visit when we are ready, but we have other things in mind.

After breakfast, Joanne and I leave the house, going in the direction of town, but after we get a little way out, we double back and head towards the trees where Bobby has built his fort.

Reaching the fort, Bobby is nowhere to be seen. I double around to the backside and Joanne goes in the other direction. Still, no Bobby. Keeping my eyes up on the surrounding trees, I am sure that Bobby will have no way of sneaking up on me.

"Bobby, where are you?" I ask. No reply.

"Come on, Bob! Stop fooling around! Get out here and talk to me," I still hear no response.

I turn towards the trees and walk until I am totally surrounded by them, my eyes trying to adjust to the change in lighting. It is much darker amongst the woodpeckers and squirrels. This is when I hear it… a sound so faint that I doubt a dog could hear it. But hear it, I did. A tree behind me goes, 'creeaak', and I know I have him.

I slowly turn towards the sound and walk in that direction, trying not to look up. It gets even harder to keep from looking up when a leaf falls to the ground right in front of me.

Then, I feel more than I see, a shape coming out of the tree directly overhead. Pretending to be scared, I tumble to the ground to keep from being tumbled. I yell, "Stop it, Bobby! Quit fooling around!"

Bobby lands on his feet, not three feet away with a roar. But after he realizes that I knew it was him, he starts laughing. "You were scared," he barks out, grinning.

"I was not," I argue. "I knew you were going to try to scare me so how could I be scared?"

"You were, too, and you know it. When I jumped out of the tree, I got a chance to see your face, and you were scared," Bobby says, his grin getting wider and wider.

He is right. I did have a frightened look on my face. But it was acting. They are going to give me an Academy Award for my performance, aren't they? "Now let's get serious so I can tell you what Joanne and I found out." I am trying to change the subject by making him think we have some hot new information for him.

"Tell me, tell me!" he reacts. "What have you got? Do we know how Nathaniel Hale gets captured?" He is practically jumping up and down with excitement.

"I think so," I explain. I really am afraid I am going to give him too much information too fast. "But wait. Have you had anything for breakfast, yet?"

"Yes. I told you there is plenty to eat around here.

I would like to eat something besides fruit."

At this, I reach into my pocket and pull out the biscuit I have hidden away for him. Grabbing it from my hands, Bobby says, "Thanks," with a full mouth. "So, you are both eating this kind of food while I am stuck in this grove of trees eating fruits and berries."

"Sorry, man," I say. "I know it must be really rough, but it looks like we are going to be able to go home soon."

"So, are you going to tell me what you have found out or are you going to make me play the guessing game?

I know, how about we play twenty questions?" By the sound of his tone, I believe Bobby is starting to get a little impatient with me. I think he can tell that I am stalling.

"Joanne and I heard… Mr. Yardshire, the man at whose house we are staying… the cousin of Nathaniel Hale. He was talking about Mr. Hale's mission. He knows all about it…" I begin, trying not to talk too fast. "I don't think he is supposed to find out… and this might be how Nathaniel gets caught."

"How did Mr. Yardshire find out?" Bobby asks.

"Uh… erm…." I stall. "I think it was in a letter that he got from a man named Ned Burton, from Virginia. Does that name mean anything to you?"

"No, it doesn't." Then, with a perplexed look on his face, Bobby asks, "Do you really think Mr. Yardshire would turn in his cousin?"

"As hard as it is to believe, yes. This morning, he was screaming about having to find a way to protect himself and his family."

"Protect? Protect him and his family from what? And isn't his cousin a part of that family?" Bobby seems more puzzled than I have ever seen him. "What in the world could Nathaniel Hale do to his cousin? I mean, first, he gets him a job in the area, then he turns him over to the Redcoats. It just doesn't seem possible."

"If this were a gameshow, I'd be handing you the cash right now," I explain. "You see, John Yardshire is afraid that if and when Mr. Hale is discovered, he, too, will be arrested as a co-conspirator. I think that he believes this Ned Burton guy is going to turn his cousin in regardless. So, he is going to try to get himself out of trouble, first. Of course, we don't know any of this for certain. We are just guessing."

Suddenly, I jump up, turning my body 180 degrees, as if I just heard a noise. I look behind where I was just standing, trying to get Bobby's eyes to follow my gaze. "Oh, no!" I shout. "I've been followed. Run!"

And, with that, I swing back around and shove Bobby backward.

Bobby, who is surprised and scared by my sudden movement, takes one shocked step back and begins to flail his arms in the air as if he were drowning. He then goes down, over the back of Joanne, who has been sneaking up behind him since we began our conversation.

Joanne stands up and throws her arms around me, howling with laughter. For me, it was paradise. The two of us, holding each other and laughing while poor

Bobby just lays there on his back, still not sure of what has just happened. Even though I feel bad for my best friend, I feel he deserves it for knocking me down before and trying to do it again today.

Finally, he stands and brushes himself off. "You guys had just better not forget who is staying in the woods, guarding the time machine."

"Oh, come on, Bobby," Joanne begins. "You know we are just getting you back for the time you knocked us down."

"Yeah," he replies in a hurt sort of way. "But I never shoved either of you to the ground."

"No," I say. "You just jump on us from the top of the trees and knock us down. We're sorry, but you gotta admit that we were just getting you back."

"I know," Bobby says in a defeated voice. "And I am sorry to act like such a baby." Then, turning to Joanne, he adds, "That was pretty good. How long have you been behind me?"

"I had just arrived," she explains. "That's how come you didn't see me. I took one careful step at a time, trying not to make any sudden movements or noises. Billy, meanwhile, did an outstanding job at keeping you in one place and distracting you so I could get into place."

"If there are no hard feelings, Joanne and I have a date back in town to get more information," I say cautiously. "Can I bring you anything when we come back?"

"Yes," he tells us. "I want you to bring Nathan here to see me. I really think we should do something to save this guy, I mean, he is one of our national heroes."

"But, if we save him," Joanne starts, "he won't be a national hero any longer. The only thing he is famous for is dying for his country, remember? And if we do anything to mess with the timeline, there is no telling what the consequences might be."

"But I can't just stand by and watch...." Bobby begins before I cut him off.

"Another thing to remember, Bobby," I say, "is that by dying for our country and not regretting his actions, he becomes a martyr."

"What's that?" he asks.

"That's a person who dies or suffers in order to give other people the will to fight or to carry on a struggle. Like Martin Luther King Jr.," Joanne adds.

"If Nathaniel Hale had not been executed and said those famous last words...." I begin.

"If he actually said those words," Joanne interjects.

"If those words were not said to have come out of his mouth, many young colonists might not have had the courage to stand up and fight for what is to become our country," I finish.

With that, our conversation is over and, after apologizing again to Bobby for the trick that we played on him one last time, Joanne and I head off for the dock.

CHAPTER 12
SAVE BOBBY

It takes us about an hour to reach the docks with the directions Mrs. Yardshire gave us earlier this morning, and I am beginning to understand why my father is always telling me that I need to get more exercise. I have the same problem with exercise as most people. My attitude. You don't think you need it… until you do.

It isn't a hot day, but Joanne has started sweating, but not nearly as much as me. She has started breathing heavily, but not as heavily as I am breathing. Yep. To put it bluntly, Joanne is not in good shape, but she is in far better shape than me.

When we reach the docks, we see many men the size of Mr. Yardshire unloading big boxes and barrels from a ship that is pulled into port. On the ship, there are several armed guards in their Red Jackets and white pants. They are wearing brown leather boots that go up to their knees or, at least, the top part of their calves.

On the dock, standing guard over the ship are several other guards in similar attire. It is almost as if they don't trust the townspeople, and I can't help but think of bank security guards in my own century. This image makes me think of an old-time police officer, which brings to mind the image of Floyd the barber on the Andy Griffith show. Thinking of his mindless stutter makes me giggle out loud.

"Shhhh," whispers Joanne. "I don't like the looks of this. Should we be here? Maybe we should leave."

"I'm sure we are allowed to be here," I say. "And there is no need to whisper. We aren't outlaws or Patriots or anything, as far as anyone can

79

tell." Then, right after I say this, I could swear at least three Redcoats look over at me. "You're right. Let's whisper," I say in a hushed tone.

"Where do you suppose the Yardshires are?" Joanne asks. "And how do you think we will ever find them?" The crowd around the pier seems to be thickening. Maybe it is only from our viewpoint or our position in the cluster of people walking, hauling the goods from the ship, or just standing around chatting, but there are a lot of people here. More than we have seen in this time period.

"I have no idea of an answer to either one of your questions," I reply. "I guess we'll have to just walk around for a while and keep our eyes open. But we really don't even know what they are wearing."

"We may have to ask one of the workers, or maybe even a soldier," she suggests. "The Yardshires are well known in these parts, and it doesn't hurt you if you have to ask for help when you don't know something." This last remark is added because Joanne always talks about how her dad refuses to ask for directions when he gets lost.

"But I want to look as if we belong here, and stopping to ask someone will really make us look different." After I say this, I look around and start to laugh.

"What's so funny," Joanne asks. "Have you lost your mind?"

"Maybe," I try to explain. "But the thought of us fitting in really makes me laugh. I mean, look around: two kids from the twenty-first century on a loading dock in the sixteenth century, surrounded by big, burly men who probably outweigh us by at least two hundred pounds. And we are trying to fit in!"

Joanne laughs at this, and we continue to walk around. At one point, Joanne stops to look at a worker who is, I admit, strikingly handsome. His arm muscles are bulging out of his shirt. And through his shirt, one can see that his chest is the perfect shape for a Charles Atlas lookalike contest. His hair is black and down to his shoulders, and his face is hairless with a boyish touch to it.

"What are we stopping for?" I ask as if I don't already know. "What is the hold up?"

"Oh, nothing," Joanne replies. Thank goodness she is kind enough to say that; my ego might have felt a little bruised if she had not. "I just had to stop and catch my breath for a moment."

That is a good answer, but I suspect that I know who took her breath away, and it isn't me. Pointing to the man that could have been a model for a workout magazine, I have to say something for my pride's sake. "Look at that guy! Why would someone want to do that to their body? It must have been really painful, and now he's sticking out all over the place. I wonder if there is a doctor that can fix that."

Pretending that she doesn't hear me, Joanne says under her breath, "Who'd want to?"

"Come on, let's go," I say, pretending that I did not just hear her comment.

That's when, as luck would have it, I am saved from any more embarrassment. Elizabeth spots us. "There they are. Over here! Over here!" she calls and she runs over to us, pulling Jacob by the shirt.

Elizabeth is wearing another dress, this one is blue with white ruffles on the neck, at the end of her long sleeves, and at the bottom of the skirt. The dress is long, and it does not allow us to see her feet. There also must have been a bustle at the bottom of the dress as it floats down and outward below her waist.

Jacob is dressed in tan pants that go down to his knees, and a clasp that keeps the pants closed at the knees. His shirt is a long-sleeved white one that is buttoned to the top and has a black ribbon tied around the collar. His shoes look too large for his feet, but they are very polished. It is easy to see the reflection of the sun shining off of them.

When the pair reaches us, Jacob pushes the hand of his sister away from his shirt and asks, "Where have you been this fine day? We have been awaiting your arrival the entire morn."

"Well," I explain. "We slept in a little bit, and then we managed to get lost on our way over here. We are new to this region."

"How could you get lost?" Elizabeth asks. "Did my mother not give you the directions?"

"Stop it, Elizabeth," Jacob insists. "They do not know the area as we do. It is not their province. They are new here." Then, turning to us, he continues, "We have been helping Father move supplies from the ships to the storage houses all morning, so we have been rather busy, anyway."

Without thinking about what I am asking, I say,

"Where is your father?"

"He is doing us a favor, right now," Jacob replies. "When he returns to the house, we are hoping to have a surprise for you."

"Yes," Elizabeth states. "You will soon have your brown-skin back."

This last statement takes me back and I find that I can think of nothing to say. No response seems to be appropriate.

"Elizabeth, I told you not to say anything to them about Father's mission," Jacob reprimands. "If he is not found now, they will be sorely disappointed."

"What do you mean, our "brown-skin?"" Joanne inquires.

"Father has gone looking to see if he can be found," Jacob explains. "There is still a chance that he cannot find him, but he has the hounds to help him, and they are good trackers."

"But this area is so big," I begin when I can speak. "How will your father even know where to begin looking?"

"I think he has been spotted," Jacob begins. "One of the townspeople told him that they had seen a brown- skin child ducking into a long line of trees beyond Mrs. Gilbert's house the other day. The trees are near a big oak tree that stands tall. He might not have even been your companion, although I believe he would have to be."

With my head still spinning from the shock of this revelation, I ask, "You mean the big tree near the road?"

"Yes, that is what I said. The big one."

Upon hearing this last part, I turn to look at Joanne, but she is already running toward the edge of town. "We've got to go," I yell to the Yardshires as I start running after her.

Jacob and Elizabeth probably know something is wrong, because they don't run after us. After a few seconds, I catch up with Joanne. "Pace yourself," I say. "We have a long run, and we will get there faster if we don't have to stop to rest every few minutes!"

She doesn't say a word to me, but she does slow her pace down a little. Not much, but just a tad. We both see the urgency of this situation, so we run without talking. That does make sense; what is there to say? Bobby is in danger!

After about two short rest breaks – not stopping, but coming to a slow trot – we come upon the line of trees near the creek. It has taken us thirty minutes, give or take, and we slow down into a fast walk.

"Let's take it kind of slow in here," Joanne says. "He might need our help, and we will not be able to lift a finger without the element of surprise."

I see the sense in this remark, so I stay at Joanne's pace, even though every fiber of my being wants to keep running until we find our friend. We duck into the trees well before reaching Bobby's fort, and we have not gone far when we hear voices. That's when our fast walk turns into a slow walk, or a crawl, or even slower.

"...and I'm going to take you back to them, boy," we hear Mr. Yardshire say.

"But they are really my friends," Bobby pleads.

"You don't have to hold my arm so tight. It's hurting me."

"They should never have treated you like an equal," the man screams. "They told me you were their friend, and you ran away from them. Of all the ungrateful things to do!"

As John Yardshire speaks, it is obvious that he just keeps getting madder and madder. "I bet those clothes you are wearing really belong to Billy. You probably are in cahoots with the band that took their parents."

"No," Bob tries to explain. "They are mine. My daddy bought and paid for them with his hard-earned money."

"Your daddy did not purchase anything," John says angrily. "If it were not for the kindness of people like the Mac family, your daddy and mom would not be living in this great colony of the crown, God save the king. Your father has no money."

"Don't talk about my daddy," Bobby says defiantly. "At least we know family loyalty. I hear you are going to turn in your cousin for spying. All to save your reputation as being loyal to the King of England. That's pretty sad."

"Why, I will...," the man starts as he raises his hand to hit Bobby. "I suspect you are a spy. Maybe even working with my cousin. That is why you disappeared from the Macs just when they needed help the most."

Before the hand can come down and strike Bobby's face, he angrily yells back at the grown man who is prepared to hit him, "It's true. You really are going to turn your cousin over to the Redcoats... your own family!"

Mr. Yardshire's voice cracks, as if in pain, as he yells, "It is done!" After this is said, the man puts his hand down and grabs Bobby's shirt with both hands. He picks our friend up off of the ground. "And now, I think I will kill you with my own hands, brown skin."

I run toward them as fast as I can. I am swinging a large branch that I have picked up off of the ground under the trees. "Mr. Yardshire, wait," I scream. "Please don't hit him."

"Why not," the man inquires. "First, these clothes he has on are obviously taken from you. Much too nice to be his. And then, he runs away from you when you and your sister need him the most." At this point, the man's face is bright red with anger, and he is practically fanning us as he swings his arms to make his point. "And one more thing," he shouts. "The things he said to me have been very disrespectful and unpleasant to my ears. He deserves to die, or at least suffer at the hand of one whom he has offended."

By this time, I am standing beside Bobby and trying to maneuver myself in between the two. "Just let me beat him," I say, not looking at Bobby. I can feel his incredulous stare, shocked at my words. "He is ours, and I don't want him to die."

"Alright, son. I will accept that. However, when you are done hurting him, I would like to get one swat in with the stock you have brought." Mr. Yardshire's face, which had turned bright red, is starting to return to its normal shade of tan.

"Okay. Let me think for a second about how I want to do this." I hold the stick out to John Yardshire and ask, "Do you think that this stick I brought will work, or do you think I need something bigger?"

The big man simply looks at the stick, nods his head, and says, "This should work."

I turn my back to Mr. Yardshire in such a way that I am now facing Bobby. "I'm sorry, Bobby," I say softly as I lift the stick over my head.

Bobby shuts his eyes and covers his head with his arms. I bring the stick down, but instead of it hitting him, I stop the motion of the stick in mid-swing. Then, I quickly turn around and give Mr. Yardshire a shove, trying to put all of the force of my weight and the stick into it.

John Yardshire is large enough that my shove doesn't even phase him. But he is so stunned by my actions that he takes one step back. He begins to flail his arms in the air and wave them to keep his balance. Before he knows what is happening to him, he is tumbling over the back of Joanne. I run past Joanne on the right and hit him with the stick.

My first swing is batted away by John's hands, as he swings them upwards in a natural, reflexive way, but my second swing lands right on target, the middle of the man's forehead. I am not sure, but it looks like I have single-handedly knocked that humongous man out cold! Well, maybe not by myself. But I am still proud of the planning that we had to do to accomplish this task.

"Give me a shot at him, Billy," Bobby says in an angry voice that I hope he never has to raise at me. "I'm the one he humiliated."

"Bobby, we don't have time for revenge," Joanne adds as she stands and brushes herself off. "We have to get into town before they hang Nathaniel Hale. Maybe we can do something to save him. Billy, get the time machine."

"She's right," I say as I turn and face my friend. "I seriously doubt they will have a long trial… if they have one at all."

Before I can turn towards the tree that has the machine buried under it, Bobby grabs me by the shoulders and envelopes me in a tight hug. "Thanks for having my back. I was really afraid he was going to hurt me."

I take a step back and look my friend in the eyes. "I know you would have done the same for me. I hope you know I would never have hit you."

Bobby nods, and I turn to the place where the machine is buried. I quickly dig it up. Bobby follows me and anxiously awaits the arrival of his jacket that we used to insulate the machine.

After I hand the jacket back to Bobby, he throws it around his waist and the three of us set off at a fast, steady pace in the direction of the town. Luckily, all three of us are so pumped full of adrenaline that we are able to make pretty good time.

Chapter 13
History Is Made, But It's Time To Go

When we arrive in town, a crowd has gathered near the town square. This must be the usual place for town meetings, because there is a platform that looks like a great place to hear or to give a speech, and the crowd seems to be facing this platform.

Bobby elects to watch what happens from the rear of the crowd, and who can blame him after all he has been through?

"Are you sure you don't want to see this up close?" I ask though I can understand how he feels. I want to help Nathan, too, but what would that do to the timeline? Would we still win the American Revolution? "This really is history in the making."

"I'd rather not," Bobby says while he hangs his head down and looks at the ground. "You guys go ahead. I'll be fine."

"If one of us stays behind, I think we should all stay behind," Joanne offers. I do agree with her and show it with a brisk nod of my head. But I am disappointed that I will have to miss the speech, especially after all we have gone through to be here.

"I am behind you, one hundred percent. We can probably hear the speech from here. I just want to know if he says what he is reported to have said," I say, trying to sound convincing.

"No way. I don't want you to miss the speech on account of me. Go ahead," Bobby says courageously.

"Bobby's right," Joanne says. "There's no sense in all of us missing this. This isn't one of my favorite events in history, anyway. Billy, you go ahead."

"What will you do if someone questions who you are?" I ask. I am thinking I might be able to talk one of them into going with me.

Bobby has a smirk on his face as he says, "I'll just call her 'Mas'er' and everything will be fine.

Joanne gets an angry look on her face and I say, "Very funny, Bob. Notice you are the only one who thinks that is funny."

Joanne shifts her gaze from Bobby to me and says, "We'll be fine. Now go quickly so you can hear what he says. Then you can come back and tell us if we missed anything."

"Okay," I finally agree in a defeated sort of way.

I turn to the front of the crowd and start heading in that direction. I have to admit that I am excited about hearing the speech. This is an opportunity that no one has witnessed since 1776.

Edging up to the crowd, I push and shove myself forward. I suppose that I get quite a few people upset with my aggressive behaviors, but, luckily, I'm small, so by the time most of the people turn to see who is bumping them, I am gone!

As I make my way to the wooden platform, I recognize from old movies what it actually is: a gallows! This isn't a speech platform. It is where they are going to hang Mr. Hale!

No, uh-uh! I did not sign up to watch someone die. I turn to get back to my friends, but the crowd has closed in so there are no openings anymore that I can use to get out. I try not to be too conspicuous as I turn my head toward the gallows. Mr. Hale is facing a small group of about five red-coated soldiers. One of the Redcoats stands above the rest, and he has on a fancier uniform with more red and gold tassels around his shoulders and four brass medals on his chest. He seems to be in charge.

"Do you, Nathan Hale, readily admit to treason against the Royal crown of England and the provinces in which you reside?" the man with the fancy uniform asks.

"I am guilty, General Howe," replies the accused.

"I, hereby, sentence you to be hanged by the neck until you are dead. Have you anything to say?" the general asks.

Mr. Hale looks afraid to be up on the scaffolds, but he holds his head high and says, "I would like to talk to a clergyman before I am executed."

"Your request is denied, Mr. Hale," the general replies. "Anything else?"

Nathan lowers his head, then raises it again as he says, "A Bible will put me at peace with my Lord."

"This request, too, is denied," the general says sternly. He looks up at the sky, then back at the crowd, and says in a loud voice, "On this morning of September 22, in the year of our Lord, 1776, Nathan Hale shall be hanged by the neck until he is dead. By the authority of the English Crown, King George the Third!"

Now I am starting to doubt that Nathan Hale is ever going to make the famous speech that inspired so many colonists to revolt against England. He is approached by two soldiers, one carrying a hood and the other, carrying nothing. The soldier without the hood takes the rope on the gallows and holds up the end, exhibiting a noose to the people standing around. He then places the noose around Nathan Hale's neck.

The soldier with the hood approaches Nathan and is about to put the hood over his head when Mr. Hale jerks his body back and shouts for everyone to hear, "I only regret that I have but one life to lose for my fellow colonists."

After hearing this, I turn and begin pushing my way through the crowd. It is difficult because it seems everyone wants to get closer and the gaps between the people seem to be getting smaller, but that doesn't matter. I continue to push. Seeing a brave man like this die is really not what I have bargained for, and I am beginning to feel a little sick to my stomach.

Before I can get out of the crowd, I hear a distinct thud. I continue to struggle to get out, and I finally reach the outer circle of onlookers. I run up to Joanne and Bobby and see that they know what has happened. Joanne is crying, and Bobby's eyes have watered up as well. That's when I realize that I, too, have tears streaming down my face.

Without saying a word, we begin walking away. We duck beside one of the buildings on the town square and see a shed in the back. Going into the storage shed, we sit down.

"That is the bravest thing that I have ever witnessed," Joanne begins, still weeping with the emotion that we all are feeling. "He just seemed so helpless up there, but he never lost his courage."

"Yes," I add. "And because he never lost his courage, he will never die. He will live on in the history books."

"But, is it fair that he should have to die like that? Without a preacher or a Bible?" Bobby joins in. "They tried to take all of his dignity away. We should have tried to do something to help."

"We already talked about this," Joanne says, sounding a little bit irritated. "If we had stopped this event from taking place, many would-be Patriots might never have realized what a noble cause they were going to be fighting for."

"And, besides," I add, "the more they try to take away his dignity, the more dignity he actually received. I hope that when I die, it can be with as much dignity as Nathan Hale."

"Yeah," Bobby finally admits. "I guess you're right. I guess this whole adventure takes some courage on our part, as well. Done is done, and throughout this voyage, we have tried to keep the timeline pure and untroubled."

"We have witnessed history being made. I think we need to have a name for our little team. What should we call ourselves?" I ask.

"How about we call ourselves the 'Time Adventures'?" Bobby suggests.

"That's good," Joanne offers. "But I think we should have a simpler name. Why don't we call ourselves… the 'Time Team'?"

At the sound of that name, we all nod our heads and agree that we will be known as the 'Time Team'. We then laugh about it for several minutes.

"Okay, guys. I am emotionally drained, and I am ready to go home," Joanne announces. "We have made new friends, and gotten some pretty cool clothes. Now, let's get out of here."

"No objection, here," I say. "But I don't want to go back to the microscope room with my body half in and half out of a cabinet. Let's try to get in the position we were in when we left and kind of get closer together." I then pull the time-traveling device out of my pocket and hand it to Joanne.

Joanne takes the device in her hands while Bobby and I get on either side of her the way we were in the microscope closet. She gives each of us a hug and says to grab her arms. We watch her as she pushes the button, turning on the power, and then pushes the time travel button that sends us to our new location. I am trying to stay awake since this is our last trip. But the blinding light returns, and, this time, I think I feel the wind on my face. Then, nothing.…

92

NEXT STOP:

DESTINATION 2.

9 798896 393542